"Can I make a sexy suggestion?" Philly asked

She cleared her throat, then continued. "How about we have a fling? It will only last while we're on the island, and will remain our secret. Once we're home, we'll go back to being friends. But for now, anything goes...."

Roman said nothing. Still the hunger in his eyes had her toes curling. Still, his hesitation spurred her on. She wanted to nail this deal...now. She didn't want Roman reneging on their agreement at a more awkward time....

"Listen," she said, stroking his chest, and watching in satisfaction as he stiffened. "Why don't we pretend to be strangers? I want you and you want me, and while we're here, we'll indulge all our sexual fantasies. No strings. And no holds barred. Deal?"

There were a few moments of silence, each one seeming like an eternity to her. Then suddenly he pulled her into his arms and kissed her roughly, frantically...thoroughly.

Finally coming up for air, he touched his forehead to hers. "I hope you don't regret this, Philly."

She wasn't going to worry about regrets. And she was determined to keep Roman so *occupied*, he wouldn't have a chance to think about them either....

Blaze™

Dear Reader,

I'm thrilled that writing *Lie with Me* has given me a chance to return to the Angelis family and finally tell Philly's story. You may have met Philly's older brothers, Kit, Nik and Theo, in the TALL, DARK... AND DANGEROUSLY HOT! miniseries I wrote for Harlequin Blaze in 2007.

Ever since she was sixteen, Philly Angelis has been in love (but most recently, in lust) with entrepreneur and CEO Roman Oliver, her brother's best friend. Only, she's not a love-struck teen anymore. Now she's a woman with goals. And her first goal is to get Roman exactly where she wants him—into her bed.

But when Roman turns her down, Philly decides drastic measures are necessary. So she travels to the island of Corfu to find a sexy Greek man who will make her forget Roman ever existed.

Philly's plan goes awry when a very jealous Roman follows her. It seems Roman has been *lying* to her about his feelings. So Philly revises her goal and uses every sensual trick she knows to seduce Roman into finally admitting the truth—that they're *fated* to *lie* together.

I hope you enjoy the adventure.

Happy reading!

Cara Summers

LIE WITH ME
Cara Summers

HARLEQUIN®

TORONTO • NEW YORK • LONDON
AMSTERDAM • PARIS • SYDNEY • HAMBURG
STOCKHOLM • ATHENS • TOKYO • MILAN • MADRID
PRAGUE • WARSAW • BUDAPEST • AUCKLAND

ISBN-13: 978-0-373-79417-1
ISBN-10:   0-373-79417-7

LIE WITH ME

ABOUT THE AUTHOR

Lie with Me is Cara Summers's thirtieth story for Harlequin Books. Cara's books have won several awards, including two Golden Leaf Awards, the Award of Excellence and a Golden Quill. Cara loves writing for the Harlequin Blaze line because it allows her to tell such a variety of stories—from Extremes and Gothic romances to an exciting adventure on the magical Greek island of Corfu. When Cara isn't involved with her characters, she teaches in the Writing Program at Syracuse University. For more information about her, visit her Web site—www.carasummers.com.

Books by Cara Summers

Prologue

SECOND THOUGHTS ambushed me, stopping me short just as I reached the door to Roman Oliver's hospital room.

It was a hell of a time to be having them, but the momentum that had fueled me to race to Saint Jude's Trauma Center at the crack of dawn was threatening to drain away with the speed of air leaving a pricked balloon.

I needed that momentum if I was going to convince Roman to make love with me.

Get a grip, Philly. You've made your decision, and once you do that, you never backslide.

That was certainly true when it came to business. Since I'd graduated from college last year I'd already implemented steps in my plan to open my pet psychic business. In addition to working part-time as a hostess in my family's restaurant, I also assisted a vet at a local animal hospital, and I'd created my own Web site. But my plan with regard to Roman Oliver was not only more immediate, it was dependent on whether or not he agreed to it.

Stop dithering. Angelis women know what they want and how to get it. And you want Roman Oliver.

Through the narrow pane of glass in the door, I could see him sitting in the chair next to his bed gazing out the window. Just looking at Roman was enough to make every molecule in my body yearn.

Why did I want him? Let me count the ways. The man was incredibly attractive—if you went for a lean, raw-boned face, tousled dark hair, a full, firm mouth and the kind of hard-muscled body that ancient sculptors had captured over and over again in bronze and marble.

And it wasn't just his looks that attracted me. There was a quiet sense of determination and purpose about him that pulled at me, too.

Something fluttered right beneath my heart. Roman Oliver, current CEO of Oliver Enterprises and my brother Kit's best friend since their freshman year in college, had been causing that "heart flutter" response in me ever since I was sixteen and he'd saved my life while we were sailing. That's when I'd developed my first big crush on him. It had been a classic case of fantasy love, existing totally in my mind and completely one-sided. After all, I was sixteen and he was an older man of twenty-two.

But in the past year, my response to Roman had changed—drastically. The dryness in my throat, the thickness in the air and the heat that flooded my senses whenever I was in his vicinity signaled clearly to me that I was way beyond the crush stage and well into lust territory where Roman was concerned. Still, I might have been able to ignore my body's responses if I hadn't become convinced the attraction I felt was reciprocated. I hadn't been imagining the heated looks Roman had sent my way when he thought I wasn't looking. And I certainly hadn't imagined what had happened in his hospital room two days ago.

Nearly a week had passed since he'd taken the nearly fatal fall that had put him in Saint Jude's Trauma Center. He'd been injured at Saint Peter's Church while saving his sister Juliana's life, and it had been three more days before he'd fully regained consciousness and three days before the doctors had been able to say with certainty that there'd been no permanent injury to his spine.

I'd come to visit him every chance I got. Before that, I'd been shy in Roman's presence. But having almost lost him had motivated me to change my ways. Then two days ago, I'd been alone in the room with him. He'd been sleeping and because I couldn't help myself—I'd slipped my hand into his just as I had when he'd been unconscious. I hadn't even known that he was awake until his fingers had suddenly tightened on mine.

Startled, I'd met his eyes, and the heat I'd seen there had more than matched what I was feeling. The sharp flood of desire was something I'd never experienced before. My whole body went into a meltdown, and my mind had emptied and filled with Roman.

"Come here." His voice had been raw, hungry, and there was a question in his tone that I'd answered by sitting down on the bed next to him. He'd moved quickly then, levering himself up and moving his free hand to the back of my neck to draw me even closer until his mouth was only a breath away from mine.

Time had seemed to slow as everything about him flooded my senses. His eyes had been so beautifully dark. Had I noticed that before? And he'd smelled of soap, simple, basic. Wonderful. I could feel the press of each one of his fingers against the skin at the back of my neck.

I'm not sure who moved first, but our mouths made contact. It wasn't a kiss really—just the gentlest brush of lips against lips. But the pleasure was so intense, the need to have more so huge that when he'd suddenly dropped his hand and drew back, I'd wanted to cry out in protest. But before I could make a sound, someone had spoken from behind me.

"Good morning, Philly. I'm beginning to believe that Roman's recovery depends on your visits."

Roman's father. I'd taken a moment to gather my thoughts before I turned to him and managed a smile.

I hadn't slept for two nights as I'd relived those torrid moments and fantasized about what might have happened if we hadn't been interrupted…

Though I'd visited him each day, we hadn't been alone again. Finally, this morning, I'd reached a decision. It was high time I took action. I wasn't a sixteen-year-old with a schoolgirl crush. I was a woman, and I knew what I wanted.

Even now, I wanted to go into the room and touch him, to strip him out of that thin hospital gown and run my hands over that smooth skin, those taut muscles—

Roman rose suddenly from the chair. Through the slightly opened back of the hospital gown, I caught a glimpse of bare buttocks before I whirled away from the door and pressed my back against the wall. Ruthlessly, I tried to gather my thoughts, and rev up my momentum. I dragged up all the arguments I'd made to myself in the past two days, mentally ticking them off on my fingers. He'd very nearly died. I might have missed my chance of making love with Roman Oliver forever. But the Fates had spared him. The Angelis family has always put a lot of store in the Fates. Surely the fact that Roman was alive was a sign that I should do something.

Not for the first time I wished that I'd inherited my aunt Cass's power to see into the future. Psychic powers run strong in the Angelis family—especially in the women. Aunt Cass believed that the power could be traced back all the way to the Oracle at Delphi. Even my three brothers possessed some kind of clairvoyance. But my psychic ability seemed limited to the work I did with animals. I'd always had a special knack for communicating with them mentally. Some people were skeptical about my special connection with animals, but because of the pets I was able to help at the vet hospital where I worked, my reputation was growing more and more.

Animals I understood. It was people I didn't always get. So I didn't have a clue about what would happen when I propositioned Roman Oliver.

Nerves knotted in my stomach. A part of me wanted to race right back home. But I was twenty-three; Roman was twenty-nine. What were we waiting for? Drawing in a deep breath, I turned, opened the door of Roman's room and walked in.

He was back in bed with most of his body discreetly covered by the sheet, and he was reading what looked to be some business papers.

"Philly." Glancing up, he sent me a smile. The kind of brotherly smile he'd been giving me for so many years. My stomach sank, but I moved toward the bed.

"Am I interrupting?"

He glanced down at the stack of papers. "A lot of things have been piling up on my desk, and I bribed my personal assistant to smuggle some work in to me." He met my eyes again. "But I have some time for my most frequent visitor."

For a moment, our eyes merely held, and I thought for an instant I saw a flicker of something. My heart leaped.

It's now or never, Philly. Go for it.

"I came here to say…I have something that I want you to know." I'd prepared a little speech. But every time I was with Roman, I had difficulty organizing my thoughts. I couldn't help remembering what had almost happened the last time we were alone in this room. What if I stopped talking? What if I just walked to the bed and pressed my mouth to his?

"Yes?"

I caught myself twisting my fingers, something I'd stopped doing when I was in junior high. I felt a sudden surge of anger at myself. Why was I still hesitating? "I came here to talk about us and about what happened two days ago just before your father walked in."

Roman opened his mouth, but I held up a hand. "Please. Let me finish. I know that we've known each other a long time. And for a lot of that time, I've had a kind of schoolgirl crush on you." *Get to the point, Philly.* "But my feelings for you have changed. I'm very attracted to you and I want to make love with you."

For a moment, Roman said nothing, and I couldn't read anything in his expression. Finally, he responded, "Philly, I want you to know that I care a great deal about you, in much the same way that I care for my sisters, Juliana and Sadie."

Pain struck—a hard sucker punch to my gut. I might not have been able to say another word if a surge of temper hadn't followed. Hands fisted on my hips, I strode toward the bed. "It wasn't brotherly affection I saw in your eyes two days ago, and I didn't imagine your mouth brushing against mine. If your father hadn't walked into the room, we would have kissed and a whole lot more."

I saw another flicker in his eyes. Of desire? Or pity?

"I'm sorry. I was afraid you might have misinterpreted that, and I should have said something sooner. I was just waking up, and I thought for a moment you were someone else. Someone I've been dating."

For a moment, I couldn't think, couldn't breathe. The second slap of pain was too consuming. It pounded into my heart like a fist.

But I didn't have to say anything—Roman was talking. I saw his lips moving, but only caught bits and pieces—

something about how he thought of me as family, loved me like a sister. And that he couldn't lead me on but it was a good thing I'd brought it up so that we could clear the air. And then he apologized.

I nearly saw red. I'd spent most of my twenty-three years learning to control my temper. But this time, I was grateful for it because it helped me deal with the pain. Roman was dead-on right about the fact that it was a good thing I'd brought the subject up. Because now I had my answer—even though it wasn't the one I'd wanted.

Pride ran deep in the Angelis family, and I didn't think I'd ever needed it more. Squaring my shoulders, I said, "I won't bother you again."

Then, somehow I made it out of the room.

ROMAN STARED at the door after it swung shut. Philly Angelis had thrown him for a loop, and he still couldn't gather his thoughts. For two days, he hadn't been able to rid his mind of the memory of what had nearly happened right in this room. He'd almost kissed her, and if he had, he wouldn't have stopped there.

He never went into a business meeting unprepared, but he hadn't been prepared for her today. If he had been, he would have handled the situation better. He wasn't even clear on what he'd said to her. The words he'd spoken had been nothing but babble in his ears because he'd had to focus all his energy on staying still when, with every fiber of his being, he'd wanted to go to her, take her into his arms and act on the proposition she'd just made him. How many times had he imagined having her beneath him, plunging into her again and again?

Now, he'd hurt her—the last thing he'd wanted. But it was for her own good, and for his. Roman raised his hands, intending to run them through his hair. When he saw they were shaking, he dropped them back down on the blanket. Something akin to fear moved through him.

No other woman had ever affected him this way. For years, he'd been guiltily lusting after Philly Angelis—ever since she was sixteen. He'd taught himself to live with the steady thrum of desire he'd felt whenever he was near her. And for years, he'd been able to control it by reminding himself that she was too young for him. But since she'd returned from college a year ago, all of his discipline and control had been slipping away. Whenever she was near, desire escalated into a raging need that bordered on pain. There'd been an incident at the Angelises' family restaurant, the Poseidon, when he was sure Kit had caught him watching Philly. Roman had seen something in Kit's eyes. A question? A warning? But then Theo and Nik had joined them, and Kit had said nothing.

But Roman didn't need a warning from Kit. Even without the age difference, he could never act on his attraction to her. The Angelises were family to him. Kit and Nik and Theo were the brothers he'd never had. Becoming sexually involved with their little sister was out of the question. Her father, Spiro, a man Roman looked on as a second father, was an old-fashioned Greek. He'd expect commitment. Marriage.

Hell, Philly would expect it. And deserve it. And Roman had long ago decided that marriage was not on his agenda. Oliver Enterprises would always be his first priority. Ever since he was a boy, he'd dreamed of running the company his father had created. But there was a price to pay. A wife and family would always suffer from neglect. He'd experienced that personally and so had his sisters. His father had buried himself in the business while they'd been growing up, and even more so after their mother's death. Roman had spent more time with his younger sisters than Mario Oliver ever had. He was now on wife number three, and she was already constantly complaining that she saw nothing of him.

I'm very attracted to you and I want to make love with you.

God. This time Roman managed to run his still-trembling hands through his hair. Words always made things more real. When she'd looked into his eyes and spoken them, he'd very nearly lost it. He could have had her right here in his hospital bed. Or on the floor. Or in the chair where he'd been sitting and fantasizing about her. It would have been wild and crazy and perhaps once would have been enough. But Roman didn't think so.

He'd done the right thing, the only thing he could do. Whatever hurt Philly had experienced today would pale in comparison to the way he'd hurt her if he acted on his feelings. She'd keep her distance now. He'd stay away from her family's restaurant and gradually the feelings would fade.

They had to.

He glanced down at the business papers he'd been reading, but it was a long time before he could actually see them.

1

One month later…

"YES, CALL ME BACK just as soon as you have some information on flights." I hung up the phone on my travel agent and turned to face my two curious cats.

Well, Pretzels was curious. And a bit apprehensive. He could always sense it when I was thinking of leaving him for any length of time. Not that I did it very often. Peanuts, his sister, had a more complacent nature. Though they looked very much alike, a pure silvery-gray with white paws, they had very different personalities.

Right now, both cats were seated on the wide window seat of the small apartment I kept in the mansion my aunt Cass had inherited from her father. The house was huge, and it took a lot of money to keep the place going, so about four years ago the family had decided to renovate it into apartments. My brothers and I each paid rent on our own places, and my dad and new stepmother, Helena lived in the gardener's cottage. When we eventually moved out, Aunt Cass could continue to make a good income by renting the apartments out.

"I'm going to go to Greece," I informed my two pets. Saying the words aloud helped make my plan more of a reality, and a little thrill moved through me. I hadn't told anyone yet, so Pretzels and Peanuts were functioning as my test audience. It was a role they often played. My family tended to be a bit protective of me, and I wasn't sure how they'd react to my trip. Of course, now that I'd made my decision, I was going to go to Greece no matter what, but I'd have a better time if they weren't worrying too much.

Pretzels immediately leaped off the window seat and joined me on the couch. His apprehension had escalated into high anxiety. I lifted him onto my lap and began to stroke him. "You'll be with Aunt Cass and Kit." I pictured first one apartment and then the other in my mind. Then I pictured Aunt Cass and Kit. Almost immediately he began to calm. "They'll take good care of you."

With a sigh, Pretzels settled himself firmly on my lap as if to keep me there. He was a bit possessive of me. Peanuts remained on the window seat cleaning her paws. I sensed she was already anticipating the extra treats she would receive from Aunt Cass and Kit.

Of all my brothers, Kit was the one who most loved animals. He had a huge dog named Ari who often stayed with me when Kit was working on one of his P.I. jobs. Luckily my cats loved Ari, and vice versa. Kit would be the primary caretaker of my animals while I was away, and Aunt Cass would serve as backup.

As soon as I told them of my plans.

Pretzels was already snoring, so I eased him off of my lap and, after stopping to scratch Peanuts behind the ears, let myself out of my apartment. The cats had taken it pretty well. I hoped the news would go as well with the rest of the family.

As I climbed the stairs to the third-floor tower room where my aunt Cass spent much of her time, I tried to gather my thoughts—something that I was finding increas-

ingly difficult to do since I'd walked out of Roman's
hospital room a month ago. I'd vowed that day that I was
going to get him out of my system once and for all. My
utter failure to accomplish that was what had triggered my
decision to go to Greece.

In the past month, Roman and I had only run into one
another once, at the wedding reception my father, Spiro,
and his new wife, Helena, had given at the Poseidon. That
had been two weeks after I'd left his hospital room for the
last time. I couldn't avoid attending my father and Helena's
party; neither could Roman. But we'd managed to steer
clear of each other.

What I couldn't shake were the feelings he stirred up
in me. All he'd had to do was walk down the steps to the
main dining room of the Poseidon, and I'd realized that I
wanted him even more desperately than I had before.
Nothing had changed. Frustrated and angry with myself,
I'd thrown myself into my work, but that hadn't helped,
either.

Dr. Wilson at the vet hospital had begun to depend on
me to help him diagnose what was troubling the animals
he saw, and recently he'd commented on the fact that I'd
seemed distracted. That's when I'd decided that drastic
action was required. I was going to Greece.

When I reached the door to the tower room, I hesitated, once more gathering my thoughts. Aunt Cass had
raised my brothers and me ever since I was four and her
husband and my mother had been taken from us in a
tragic boating accident. In many ways, she was the only
mother I'd ever known.

The door swung open and Aunt Cass smiled. "I've been
expecting you."

I glanced over to a sitting area and spotted a teapot and

cups on the coffee table. Of course she'd been expecting me. Aunt Cass had been one of the most well-known and successful psychics in the San Francisco area even before my older brother Nik got himself engaged to J. C. Reilly, the mayor's daughter, and her business had increased by almost fifty percent.

Next to the tea tray, I saw the crystals that Aunt Cass frequently used to help her see into the future. Over a month ago she'd foreseen the dangerous adventure that my brothers were going to have on one fateful weekend and she'd known that they would each meet the woman they were destined for.

Oddly enough, my brothers' good fortune in finding their true loves had had a ripple effect on other members of the Angelis family. My dad had finally gotten engaged to Helena, and my aunt Cass had met and begun to date two men—Mason Leone, who headed up security for the Oliver family, and Charlie Galvin, the police commissioner. Roman and I seemed to be the only ones romantically unaffected by the events of that weekend.

Aunt Cass drew me over to the couch. While she poured tea, she said, "You're hurting."

"Yes." I took the cup she handed me and set it down. "But I don't want to be. I hate the fact that I am."

"This is about Roman."

I glanced at the crystals, then at Aunt Cass. "You know."

She nodded as she sipped tea from her cup. "All wounds heal."

I opened my mouth and then shut it. If anyone had the experience of that, Aunt Cass did. She'd lost her husband, Demetrius, the one true love of her life, nineteen years ago. And her son, Dino, had been gone for two years serving in the navy.

"Okay. I can accept that. But I want to hurry the healing along. I can't concentrate. I mixed up two dinner reservations at the Poseidon last night. And this morning I couldn't focus when Mrs. Trumble brought her cat, Esmerelda, in to see Dr. Wilson. Neither she nor Esmerelda were happy campers when they left, and Dr. Wilson had already told me that I seem distracted lately. I want to get Roman Oliver out of my system and get on with my life."

With a smile, Aunt Cass studied me. "Of all Penelope's children, you've always been the most impatient. Have you told Roman how you feel about him?"

"Yes. A month ago, I told him I wanted to make love with him."

"Of course you did," Aunt Cass murmured. "You're always so decisive."

I looked at her then and for the first time I saw a trace of uncertainty in her eyes. Aunt Cass never seemed to be uncertain. "What is it? Do you think I did the wrong thing?"

"No, I wasn't thinking about you. I was thinking that I wish I could make decisions and act on them as easily as you do."

"This is about Mason Leone and Charlie Galvin, isn't it?"

Cass sighed. "I can't keep juggling them forever—it's not fair. And I can't seem to see anything in the crystals."

I studied my aunt with interest. She was blushing, and she actually looked flustered. I took both of her hands in mine. "I don't think you should pressure yourself. You haven't dated anyone since Uncle Demetrius died. Take your time. Enjoy both of them. I'll bet that's why you're not seeing anything in the crystals. When the time is right, you will."

Cass leaned over to kiss my cheek. "Thank you. Now tell me more about Roman. What did he say when you told him you wanted to make love with him?"

Temper and frustration streamed through me as it did

whenever I let myself recall what had happened in Roman's hospital room that day. Rising, I strode to a space near one of the long, narrow windows where I could pace. "He said that his feelings for me were brotherly. And even if they weren't, we couldn't have a...sexual relationship because I'm Kit's sister—or something stupid like that. He didn't want to hurt me."

"It sounds like he cares a great deal for you."

I turned and strode back to the sofa. "He cares for me the way he cares for his sisters. And I know what they mean to him. Sadie and Juliana have told me how he stepped in and tried to fill their parents' shoes after their mother died. They hardly ever saw their father, but Roman was always there for them. The problem is that my feelings for him aren't sisterly at all. They never have been. And I refuse to be the kind of woman who spends her life pining away for a man who doesn't want her. Stuff that."

Aunt Cass picked up her tea and took a sip. "So what's your plan?"

For the first time since I'd entered the room, I felt some of my tension ease. Of course, Aunt Cass would know I had a plan. I sat back down on the couch next to her. "I've decided to go to Greece and have a fling with a sexy Greek man."

Aunt Cass didn't bat an eye. "Why Greece?"

I leaned forward. "Because that's where you and mom found Uncle Demetrius and Dad. It was love at first sight. And that's where Dad met Helena, so there must be something magical about Greece when it comes to our family. I figure that if anything can get me out of this rut I've fallen into with Roman, a trip to Greece will do it."

Cass took another sip of tea, and this time I joined her.

"So you want to go to Greece to find your true love."

I frowned. "No way. I just want to find someone very

sexy to have a fling with so that I can forget Roman Oliver. I spoke with a travel agent today and she's looking for a cheap flight. The sooner I get this taken care of, the better."

CASS ANGELIS LEANED back and once again studied her niece. How wonderful that Philly's plan coincided so perfectly with her own. A little vacation, a trip to Greece, was just what she'd seen in her crystals last night. "I have a suggestion. Why don't I call your father's cousin Miranda? She operates a little hotel—the Villa Prospero—along the coastline of Corfu."

Philly's eyes lit up. "Isn't that the place that Dad and Helena just visited on their honeymoon?"

Cass nodded. "I'm sure she'd love to have you." And being family, Cass knew that Miranda would look out for Philly. Her niece had a tendency to rush headlong into things. And Philly's father and brothers would feel better about the trip if she visited family.

"How soon can I leave?"

Cass shook her head and smiled. "You never were one to let the grass grow under your feet. As soon as I check with Miranda, you can book your flight."

Philly wrapped her arms around Cass and hugged her hard. "Thanks, Aunt Cass."

Once her niece had left, Cass picked up a few of the crystals that had been sitting on the table. She could only hope that she hadn't made a mistake in suggesting the Villa Prospero to Philly. At midnight, she'd seen in the crystals Philly standing on a white sand beach. But she'd also seen blood and sensed danger —much the same things she'd seen a month ago for her nephews.

But Cass had also sensed very strongly that Philly was meant to go to Corfu. In the mists that had pulsed and eddied in the depths of the crystals, she'd glimpsed other images—a white bird soaring into a blue sky, and a man she'd recognized immediately. She suspected that he was the one Philly was fated for. But both of them would have to decide if they would accept what the Fates were offering.

Tears pricked at the back of Cass's eyes. If they did, Philly would find her true love in Greece just as she and Penelope had.

WITH A FRUSTRATED SIGH, Roman dropped the papers on his desk. This was the third time he'd tried to read through Gianni Stassis's business plan and the third time he'd drifted off in his mind.

He'd been out of the hospital for a month and physically, he was almost back to normal. There'd been no permanent nerve damage from the fall, and the doctors were amazed at how quickly his body had responded to therapy. In another month or two, he'd be able to beat his sister Sadie at tennis again. In the interim, she was thoroughly enjoying each one of her victories, and the exercise was good for him.

The problem was, his mental recovery seemed to be lagging behind his physical recovery. He couldn't concentrate. Running his hands through his hair, Roman leaned back in his chair.

Working with his father and eventually running Oliver Enterprises had always been his dream. The company dealt primarily in commercial real-estate development and before his accident, he'd been pouring every spare minute of his time into the project that Stassis, a Greek entrepreneur, had proposed to him. Even though he'd been working with his father almost 24/7 to close a deal for a prime strip of land in Orange County, he'd found time for the Stassis proposal. It involved Oliver Enterprises and Stassis Ltd. acquiring a stake in a select number of small independently operated Greek hotels. They would help them modernize and then share in a percentage of the profits. Within five years, they hoped to own a string of small exclusive hotels throughout the Greek Islands.

If he and Stassis could come to terms, this would be the first time that Oliver Enterprises would be operating outside of the United States. Roman's goal had been to take the company global for some time, and the project had been his baby. He didn't just want to run the company his father had founded, he wanted to expand it.

He'd been excited about the project with Gianni Stassis, confident of its success, and now, when it was close to coming together, he couldn't seem to drum up the same level of enthusiasm he'd had before.

Roman picked up a paperweight, tossed it into the air and caught it. Letting out a frustrated breath, he stifled the urge to throw it at the wall. It wasn't his damn fall that was to blame for his current situation. It was Philly Angelis.

A month had passed and he couldn't get her words out of his mind. What had possessed her to walk into his hospital room that day and tell him that she wanted to make love with him?

Before that, he'd been able to convince himself that she was too young, that having her was out of the question. Before she'd spoken those words, he'd been able to find happiness and total satisfaction in his work. He glanced around his office. For as long as he could remember, this was where he'd wanted to be. Now he was restless, having trouble focusing, and nothing he'd tried so far had seemed to help.

His gaze shifted involuntarily to the group of photos he had on his desk. There were various shots of his family and the Angelis family. He'd removed the one snapshot he'd always had there of Philly. Out of sight, out of mind had been his thought.

That hadn't worked. Staying away from her family's restaurant hadn't worked, either. Except for the celebration that Spiro and Helena had thrown when they'd returned from their honeymoon, he hadn't been to the Poseidon. Philly frequently filled in as hostess, and there was no telling when she might be there. Dammit, he missed it— the laughter, the music, the opportunity to hang out with Kit and his brothers.

Be honest. You miss the chance of running into Philly, too.

It wasn't as though he could hang out with his sisters, either. Sadie was spending her days with Theo Angelis, and Juliana spent as much time as she could with her fiancé, Paulo Carlucci. Roman went home each night to an empty apartment and tried to bury himself in work that he couldn't find the same satisfaction in that he did before.

He'd even thought of calling another woman. Though he'd never dated anyone seriously, there were several women who would be more than willing to share drinks or dinner followed by some satisfying and uncomplicated sex. The problem was that he couldn't work up the enthusiasm for that, either.

The bigger problem was that he couldn't get Philly's proposition out of his mind. Nor could he get rid of the image of her standing there—those wide brown eyes, that dark hair. It had curled when she was younger, but now she wore it in one of those sleek, chin-length cuts that made a man want to run his hands through it. There was a passion in her that lurked so near the surface, threatening at any moment to break through. What man in his right mind wouldn't want to be there when it finally did?

Roman glanced at the paperweight again and gave

serious thought to throwing it. Or perhaps the better
solution to his frustration was to simply take Philly up on
her offer. Maybe if he made love to her once, he could get
her out of his system. He'd almost convinced himself that
that was a reasonable alternative—perhaps the only one—
when there was a knock on his door, and Kit Angelis
strolled in.

"Long time, no see."

Roman watched Kit settle himself in a chair and felt like
the worst kind of heel. They had been fast friends ever
since Kit had also strolled into their dorm room that first
day of college. And a month ago, when he'd taken that fall
at Saint Peter's Church and had also fallen under suspicion
of murder and kidnapping, Kit and his brothers had
worked nonstop to clear his name and protect his family.
He owed Kit. He owed Nik and Theo too. And having a
one-night stand with their little sister was no way to repay
what he owed.

"Nik and Theo and I were thinking that you might have
had a relapse, but you look fit enough to me."

"I am." Roman willed himself to relax. Kit couldn't
possibly know just what he'd been thinking. "I've just
been busy."

"Good. But just the same, I'm here on a search-and-
rescue mission. My brothers and I are planning a fishing
weekend—men only—at my grandfather's fishing cabin.
We may even talk Dad into joining us. Interested?"

Roman smiled. "Absolutely." It might be just the ticket
to get him back on track. It certainly appealed more than
spending the weekend at the office or in his empty apartment. "How are you getting away from your women?"
Each of the Angelis brothers now had a special woman in
their lives, and from the looks of it, a permanent one.

They'd all met their significant others during the weekend when they'd literally saved his family.

"Easy." Kit shot him a grin. "They have a wedding to shop for. J.C. and Nik are tying the knot on Thanksgiving weekend. According to Drew, that doesn't give them nearly enough time to register for gifts and decide on flowers."

It had been so long since he'd dropped in at the Poseidon that Roman hadn't given much thought to Nik's upcoming wedding. He didn't suppose it would be long before Kit would give Drew a ring. And Theo and his sister Sadie would probably follow their lead. He'd never in his life seen men fall so hard and fast as the Angelis men had and all in the space of one weekend.

"When Philly heard about the girls-only shopping weekend, she nearly postponed her trip."

Every muscle in Roman's body tightened. "Her trip?"

Kit pointed a finger at him. "See? You really are out of touch. Philly's going to Greece."

Roman frowned. "Why?"

"That's what we all asked her." Chuckling, Kit leaned back in his chair. "You know the story about how my mom and dad and my aunt Cass and uncle Demetrius met on a beach in Greece and fell in love at first sight?"

Roman nodded. The story had become a sort of legend in the Angelis family. Spiro and Demetrius had left Greece and followed Cass and Penelope back to San Francisco.

"My dad met Helena in Greece, too."

He'd met her at the five-star restaurant where she'd been the head chef, Roman recalled. Spiro Angelis had persuaded her to come back by promising to open a similar restaurant on the top floor of the more casual Poseidon.

"So Philly has this idea that it's high time she followed in the family tradition. She's cut her hair, splurged on a new wardrobe, and she's off to Greece to find her true love."

"That's crazy!" Roman quickly rose to his feet. "Aren't you going to stop her?"

Kit shot him a quizzical look. "Trying to stop Philly once she's made up her mind is a bit like trying to stop a runaway train. But you can relax. Aunt Cass has the situation under control. She's arranged for Philly to stay at a small hotel on Corfu that's run by my dad's cousin Miranda Kostas. Philly will be perfectly safe. Helena says that Miranda is a very traditional Greek woman. Her own marriage was even arranged. She's not likely to let Philly stray too far to the wild side."

Right, Roman thought as he sat down in his chair. He was overreacting. But in his mind he saw Philly walking up to some handsome Greek and saying, "I want to make love with you."

2

THE MOMENT I STEPPED OUT of the taxi onto the crunchy white gravel path that wound its way to the Villa Prospero, I knew that I had made the right decision in coming to Greece.

My driver made a sweeping gesture with his hand. "You'll see the villa as soon as you walk around that curve."

I tried to be patient as he opened the trunk and began to unload my luggage. Now that I was here, I wanted to get started on the rest of my life—the part that I'd named Post Roman. I'd cut my hair and my brother Kit's fiancée, Drew, who was a dress designer, had helped me select a new sexy wardrobe. I barely recognized myself when I looked in the mirror.

I'd also done my homework and discovered that Corfu was believed by many to be the setting of Shakespeare's *The Tempest*—hence, the name of Miranda Kostas's hotel. The island was located off the west coast of Greece on the Ionian Sea.

I'd flown into Corfu Town, which was in the middle of the island across from the mainland of Greece. To reach the Villa Prospero, I'd hired a driver to take me to the other side of the island where the rugged coastline bordered the Ionian Sea.

My driver was an endless source of information, most

of it gossip about the Castello Corli, which sat atop a cliff about two miles away from the Villa Prospero. Venetians had built the castle in the fourteenth century—thus, the Italian name. Below the fortresslike walls, there were a series of caves that were reputed to have been used by smugglers for hundreds of years. However, according to my very talkative driver, what the Castello Corli was famous for now were the extravagant biannual parties that its billionaire owner, Andre Magellan, threw. One of his famous soirees was due to take place in three days.

"You may actually meet some movie stars walking along the beach," my mustachioed driver had said to me. "Or a member of royalty. When Andre Magellan throws one of his parties, the Castello Corli becomes a destination for the rich and the famous."

Magellan's family had supposedly been bankers in Rome for centuries. But local rumor had it that Andre was a spoiled playboy who expended all of his energy on living an opulent lifestyle and only visited his family's banks to make withdrawals.

By the time my driver had unloaded my luggage and I'd paid him, thanking him again for a very informative ride, I was itching to get to the villa and begin my Grecian adventure. I hurried along the narrow lane, then stopped short as soon as I went around that first curve. Just as the driver had promised, the Villa Prospero had come into view to my right. Color was everywhere— from the ivy and roses that draped over pink stucco to the riot of flowers that edged the path to the front of the small hotel.

The building itself was two-storied and tucked into a hillside. Parked right in front of the entrance was a sporty red convertible. The terrain to my left was rugged, thick with cypresses and fell away steeply. Through the trees, I spotted a serpentine trail that wound its way to a brilliant expanse of turquoise-blue sea. As colorful as the villa was, it was the sea that pulled at me.

I stood for a moment torn between following my impulse to take that winding path down to the beach and checking in with my cousin Miranda. In the end, family obligation won. After all, she was expecting me. I couldn't let her worry.

The ground floor was bordered by a wide terrace with several porticoes opening into the lobby. I crossed to one of them. At first I thought the lobby was deserted; there was no one behind the small reception desk. But then I heard the angry voice.

"I demand to speak with your son Alexi."

"He's not here right now, Mr. Magellan."

Peeking through the open portico, I could see two figures to my right. I recognized my cousin Miranda from the photos Helena had shown me. Her voice was calm, pleasant, professional, but the tension in her body contrasted sharply with her tone. Miranda had the kind of face that medieval artists had captured in their portrayals of the Madonna. She wore a tailored white blouse, a black skirt and sensible shoes. Her hair was pulled back in a ballerina's knot and gold hoops winked at her ears. She was average height, but the way Mr. Magellan was towering over her made her seem tiny.

I had no doubt that I was also getting an up-close-and-personal view of the rich, flamboyant playboy that my driver had described to me in such great detail. Magellan's red print shirt and matching red slacks were made even more dramatic by the way he stood in front of my cousin, his hands fisted at his sides. Diamonds glittered from his watch and a ring on his pinkie.

"Of course he's not here. Even as we speak, he's probably trespassing on my land again. It has to stop. I've warned him more than once. And I don't want him poking around in the caves, either. They're dangerous—that's why they're posted. I should think as his mother, you'd see to it that he doesn't go there."

"You don't understand. One of Alexi's cats is missing—Caliban. Alexi just wants to—"

"I don't give a damn about his cats or his fixation on them." Magellan's voice had grown shrill with temper. "I've warned him. If either of those cats are seen anywhere on the grounds of the Castello Corli, my men have orders to shoot them."

"No, please, don't hurt them." Miranda pressed a hand to her chest. "I'll speak to Alexi."

"I'm filing a complaint with the police. If your son trespasses one more time, I'll have him arrested."

Anger flared inside me at the callous way he spoke of Alexi and the cats. I knew from Helena and my dad that my cousin Alexi was eighteen and had always been a bit slow in school. But since his father had died three years ago, he'd become quite good at helping his mother run the hotel.

Fueled by my temper, I was about to move into the lobby and give Mr. Andre Magellan a piece of my mind when he whirled and strode out through the main entrance. He vaulted over the door into the sporty red car. An instant later, tires squealed and gravel sprayed as he raced away.

The lobby was empty when I turned back. To my left, doors opened onto a sunny terrace where lunch was being served, and every table was filled. Helena had raved about the cuisine at the Villa Prospero, and it seemed that the current guests were in agreement. Miranda was now serving dishes from a loaded tray. I hated to interrupt her, so I wandered around the large, airy room. There was a small gift shop that opened off the lobby, and through its open door I caught a glimpse of glass cases as well as racks of T-shirts and wide-brimmed hats.

A young woman entered from yet another door. She, too, carried a loaded tray. The moment she saw me she paused and said, "I'll be with you in a moment."

Her English was heavily accented, but she meant what she said. She returned to the lobby just as soon as she'd served a table of four.

"Sorry. You have a reservation?"

"I believe so. I'm Philly Angelis." Her name tag said that she was Demetria.

"Oh, Ms. Angelis." A smile warmed her whole face. "Welcome to the Villa Prospero. Mrs. Kostas is expecting you."

Over her shoulder, I could see Miranda chatting with the guests at a table for two as she cleared plates and cups.

"I'll get her," Demetria said.

"No, I can see she's busy. And you're busy, too. Why don't I just leave my luggage here and go for a walk until things settle a bit."

Relief swam in her eyes. "Are you sure? We're short-handed today because Alexi hasn't shown up yet."

I smiled at the young girl. "I'm positive. The sea is calling me. I thought I saw a path down to the beach."

"Yes. Just go to the end of the gravel drive and turn right."

With a final smile, I turned and after stopping briefly to get my camera out of my suitcase, I hurried out of the lobby. I believed in following my impulses, and something was pulling me to the beach, in much the same way that something had drawn me to Greece.

Of course, sometimes my acting on impulse had gotten

me into trouble. A prime example was the day Roman had saved me from drowning. I was sixteen and decided I had to go for a sail. Right then. It had been a boring, rainy day at my grandfather's fishing cabin. My brothers and Roman and my dad had been whiling away the hours with a game of poker. Roman had been winning, of course. The moment the sun had come out, I'd announced my intention to take Nik's boat out. Then I'd hurried down to the dock before anyone could object.

I'd wanted to sail alone, but Roman followed and asked if he could join me.

Before that, I'd always thought of Roman as just an additional brother, but everything changed once the storm came up. It was so sudden and so severe that the boat had capsized almost immediately. Once in the water, I'd felt a huge wave pick me up and toss me. I'd barely had time to catch a breath before I was pulled under. Dizzy and disoriented, I wasn't sure which way to swim to get to the surface. Panic had streamed through me, and I'd felt my lungs begin to burn. Then a pair of strong hands had gripped me, and seconds later Roman and I broke the surface. The water was rough and another wave had crashed over us. When we'd surfaced again, his voice had been calm as he told me to put my arms around his neck and lie on top of his back. I did, and he'd struck out toward shore. Though waves had tossed us and dragged us both under several times before we finally reached the beach, I'd never once doubted that we would both make it.

When I felt the now-familiar band of pain tighten around my heart, I stopped in my tracks and swore under my breath. I had not come to Greece to think about Roman Oliver. I had come to solve my "Roman problem" once and for all. And I would. I knew it in the same way that I often "knew" things about the animals I worked with.

The path to the sea was narrow and sloped gently as it zigged and zagged its way down the steep hill. I'd only been walking for a short time before I realized that it was going to take a while to reach my destination. I was tempted to just forget the path and strike out on a more direct route through the trees. But it wouldn't do to get lost on my first day in Corfu.

Then I rounded a sharp corner and caught sight of a wide, crescent-shaped beach and the vast stretch of the crystalline blue Ionian Sea. There was no sound other than the breeze rustling through the trees and the distant push of waves against rocks.

I raised my camera and focused the lens. The deserted stretch of white sand was tucked snugly between two rocky promontories that stretched far out into the water. Waves broke frothy and white against the rocks. I took a few shots. Beyond the far promontory, the terrain changed abruptly from wooded hillside to a cliff face of solid rock that shot straight up to form a fortress wall and two towers. It had to be the Castello Corli.

As I snapped more photos, I felt transported to a much earlier time, and I thought fancifully of the castle that Princess Aurora slept in for one hundred years after she'd pricked her finger. Because of its location between Italy and the Greek mainland, Corfu had always had strategic importance. I recalled what my driver had said about the Castello Corli being built in the fourteenth century when the Venetians had ruled the island, and I could see the Italian influence in the design of the towers. My driver had said that the estate's current villa dated from the turn of the century and had been reno-vated ten years ago by Andre Magellan's parents, and then presented to him on his birthday. I zoomed in with my telephoto lens, but even then, I could see nothing past the towers.

Suddenly my attention was caught by a large white bird that flew out of one of the towers and soared upward in wide circles. I had no idea what its species was, but an odd mix of fear and excitement moved through me. Perhaps I was still being influenced by the enchanted appearance of the Castello, but the white bird made me think of the numerous calls to adventure that populated so many fairy tales.

Silly, I said to myself. But I knew better. Hadn't I known all along that I was meant to come to Greece? More than ever I was convinced that the Fates had brought me here.

Once the bird had disappeared inland, I lowered my camera and continued to follow the frustrating, snakelike path. Gradually, the vegetation thinned. Cypresses and pines were replaced by boulders and rocks. As I rounded yet another sharp curve, I caught another glimpse of the crescent-shaped beach. It was no longer deserted. There were two men standing near the far promontory near the Castello.

Curious, I raised my camera and focused the lens. It was only as I zoomed in that I spotted the cat. It was so pale in color that it nearly blended into the white sand, and it was circling the two men. Not happy, I thought. And female. The cat had to be seriously agitated for me to be able to sense so much over such a distance. She reminded me a bit of Pretzels. What was the source of her worry?

I shifted my attention back to the two men. They were deep in conversation, and from the gestures the younger man was making, it appeared to be a heated one. He looked to be in his late teens. The older man pointed to the cell phone he had in his hand. Both men were of medium height and wearing sunglasses and shorts, and both carried backpacks, but that's where the resemblance stopped. The older man had a more portly build. He wore a T-shirt, hiking boots and a wide-brimmed hat that cast his face in shadow. A pair of binoculars was slung over one shoulder.

He turned and took a few steps in my direction, but the other man grabbed his arm and stopped him. The younger man had an athletically toned body, and sun glinted off a medal he wore around his neck.

The cat was circling them now, growing more agitated. The younger man squatted, and when she went to him, he stroked her. But she backed away. It wasn't soothing that she was after.

The man in the hat was hurrying along the beach now in my direction. The other man rose, ran after him, then grabbed his arm and jerked him around. The argument escalated, and suddenly, the younger man shoved the older man to the ground. When he fell, he missed the cat by inches.

Concern for the animal filled me, and lowering my camera, I gave up on the path and began to make my way down the rugged hillside in a more direct route to the beach. By the time I reached it, my view of the two men and the cat was blocked by the rocks that bordered the little cove on the Villa Prospero's side.

I felt the cat before she appeared around a boulder. Her emotions slammed into me with enough force to stop me in my tracks. The agitation I'd sensed earlier in her had given way to terror, urgency. In my head I saw a bright red color. I squatted, tried to calm my mind and waited for her to come to me. She did, pausing when she was only a few feet away.

Slowly, I held out my hand. *I'm Philly. I'm a friend.*

Most often when I communicated with animals, I did it mentally. I thought what I wanted them to know—sometimes in words, other times in images, depending on the initial way the animal communicated with me.

She was a beauty—nearly pure white, and her eyes a pearly mix of gray and green. Without coming any closer, she studied me in much the same way I was studying her. The emotions rolling through her were chaotic, and I couldn't get a clear image.

What's your name?

Ariel.

I'd heard the word in my mind as clearly as if she'd said it aloud. With a name like Ariel, I bet she was one of Alexi's cats. I recalled Miranda had mentioned the name of the other—the one that was missing. Caliban.

Help.

This time I caught an image. A white cat lying still in a shadowy place. Bigger than Ariel, I thought. I caught the gleam of his eyes before everything went red.

Ariel turned and raced back toward the boulders.

When she paused to glance back, I was already on my feet and heading after her. She had an easier time of climbing down the rocks than I did. After slipping for the second time, I thought, *Slow down.*

Ariel paused and waited for me. The moment I joined her, she began to run again, and I followed her lead. I was beginning to feel the same overpowering sense of urgency and fear that I was getting from her. The two men who'd been with her at the far end of the beach were gone. It wasn't until I reached the center of the crescent that I realized I was wrong. One of them was still there—lying on the sand. I broke into a sprint.

I was out of breath when I finally reached the man. As I dropped to my knees, my mind registered details. He was the older of the two men I'd seen. His wide-brimmed hat had fallen off, and he was lying faceup, the backpack and binoculars at his side. But my eyes were riveted to the hole in the side of his head, and the large red stain on the white sand. My heart was racing and not from the run. I wasn't a forensic scientist, but it looked like a bullet hole to me. Wouldn't I have heard the shot?

My stomach was in free fall, my hand shaking as I did what I'd seen people do on countless TV shows. I put two fingers to the side of his neck and felt for a pulse.

Nothing.

I felt myself going numb. When an insect hummed past my cheek, I brushed at it absently. Then out of the corner of my eye, I saw Ariel, standing, watching me. Waiting. Worrying.

Help.

This was no time to go numb. *I can't help him. He's dead.*

Once again an image flashed into my mind—the white cat. There were fewer shadows this time because of dappled sunlight, so I caught more details. Next to the cat was what appeared to be the remains of a small animal. A bird? And I made out a puddle of water. Even as the image faded, questions poured into my mind. What was Ariel trying to tell me? Was the other cat the one that was missing? And what was her relationship to the dead man? Had she witnessed what had happened to him? Where was the younger man who'd stroked her and shoved this man to the ground?

The list of questions would have gone on if I hadn't heard another insect hum by. This time I also heard a *ping* and I glanced in the direction of a nearby boulder. Then I heard yet another hum and saw sand erupt inches away from Ariel.

Shock threatened to numb me again. Someone was

shooting at us. He had to be using a silencer. That was why I hadn't heard a shot.

Run.

Ariel took off first, racing toward the foot of the hill. A second later she'd leaped across rocks and disappeared into the trees. I was about three beats behind her and not quite as fleet of foot. But that gave me time to spot the flash of reflected sunlight from the woods bordering the Castello Corli.

Ariel! Wait. I scrambled over the rocks and raced after her into the cypresses.

CASS ANGELIS STOPPED pacing the moment the knock sounded on her door. When she opened it and saw Kit, some of her tension eased.

He hugged her soundly, then moved to the tea tray she'd set up near the couches. He never drank the tea, but he'd already popped one of the finger sandwiches into his mouth. "Mission accomplished," he mumbled around it. "Roman's plane should be touching down in Corfu Town as we speak."

"Good."

He glanced at Cass, studying her for a moment. Then he sat down on one of the couches and gestured for her to join him. "Everything's going just the way we planned. Philly's in Corfu, and Roman has followed her. What's worrying you?"

Of all of her nephews, Kit was the one who could always read her the most clearly. She sat next to him and picked up one of her crystals. "This morning I was out at the pond." Kit knew that she usually went there at sunrise—visions often formed for her in the water. "I saw more—Philly and Roman standing on white sand and there was a castle in the distance. I saw a white cat, and there was blood on the sand. It's the second time I've seen blood."

Kit frowned. "Philly's or Roman's?"

Cass shook her head. "No. But they're headed into danger. I sensed that before. And that cat—if there's an animal in the middle of it, your sister is going to get involved."

Kit took one of her hands. "Maybe an adventure is just what the two of them need. Look at Nik and J.C., Theo and Sadie, Drew and me—we were all in a lot of danger the weekend we fell in love. You keep reading the crystals, and I'll keep in touch with Roman. If things get serious, I'll go over and give them some backup."

Cass smiled at her nephew. "You always know what to say to make me feel better."

He leaned closer and kissed her cheek. "Funny—you have the same effect on me." Then he grabbed another sandwich. "Mason said to give you his best."

Cass's heart skipped a beat. "You saw him?"

"He was at the Poseidon last night. I think he was hoping to run into you."

Cass felt the heat rise in her cheeks. She'd been attending a fund-raiser for the mayor with Charlie Galvin.

"Sooner or later you're going to have to decide between those two men."

"I can't. I can see that Roman and Philly are meant to be together. And I knew the moment I saw Demetrius that he was the one for me. But with Charlie and Mason, I can't tell—I like them both. They're very different. Charlie is so outgoing while Mason is reserved. Philly says to give it time and I'll know. But maybe I'm not meant to be with either of them."

Kit squeezed his aunt's hand. "You'll figure it out. You always do."

3

ROMAN STEPPED OUT of the car he'd hired in Corfu Town. A sense of urgency had been growing in him ever since his plane had touched down. His decision to come to Greece had been made shortly after Kit had left his office two days ago. The trip *was* business related. Meeting personally with Gianni Stassis in Athens would allow him to finalize the details of their project. Oliver–Stassis Ltd. would be officially launched, and his dream of taking Oliver Enterprises into the global market would be realized. But Roman wasn't a man who liked to lie to himself. He'd also come to Greece to check on Philly.

If his plane had been on time, he would have landed at the Corfu airport before Philly. His plan had been to have a reasonable talk with her and persuade her to go back to San Francisco. Or if that didn't suit her, he'd take her with him to Athens for his business meeting with Stassis. At least he could keep an eye on her there.

Exactly what he was going to say to her still hadn't come to him yet, even though he'd had plenty of time to think about it on the long flight. But he was a first-rate negotiator. Surely he could make Philly see the risk in coming to Greece to make love with a perfect stranger. And he had no doubt that was what she intended to do. A mix of fear and frustration streamed through him. She might be propositioning someone right now.

When his flight had been delayed, he'd had to reschedule his meeting with Gianni Stassis and switch to plan B—follow Philly to the Villa Prospero. The driver he'd hired had promised in broken and minimal English that he knew exactly where it was. Now, after a two-hour drive, the hotel was nowhere in sight.

Tamping down his temper and his growing sense that Philly had already gotten into some kind of trouble, Roman paid the driver, tipping him generously, and asked, "The villa?"

For a moment, the driver looked puzzled.

Roman made a sweeping gesture with one hand and repeated the question.

This time the driver shot him a beaming smile, motioned for Roman to follow and then grabbed his carry-on and led the way up the white-graveled driveway. Around the first curve, Roman spotted the small hotel and breathed a sigh of relief. Maybe his luck was turning. Nodding his thanks to the driver, he shouldered his bag and strode up the drive.

Once inside the lobby, he let his gaze sweep the room. It was a pleasant airy space, with doors opening onto a sunny terrace where people were enjoying food and drinks. In the distance he caught a glimpse of an incredibly blue sea.

He turned his attention to a young girl behind the registration desk and read her name tag. He prayed that Demetria's English was better than his driver's. When he smiled at her, she responded by directing a worried glance at his bag.

"Welcome to the Villa Prospero. Do you have a reservation?"

He hadn't made one because he'd expected to settle things with Philly in Corfu Town. Setting his bag down, he turned up the wattage on his smile. "No, I'm sorry—my plans changed at the last moment. I'm afraid I was depending on luck to get a room. I've heard so many good things about the Villa Prospero."

Concern filled her eyes. "I'm so sorry, but we're full. There's a huge party going on at the Castello Corli the day after tomorrow, and we've taken in the overflow. I could try to find you a room in the village."

When she reached for the phone, Roman stopped her. "That won't be necessary. I actually came to surprise someone—Ms. Philly Angelis. Is she here?"

"No."

Roman frowned. "She should have arrived by now."

"She has, about an hour ago. Mrs. Kostas and I were in the middle of serving lunch, so Ms. Angelis went for a walk on the beach."

Just the word *beach* had an image forming in his mind of Philly rolling around in the sand with some strange man. "How do I get there?"

For the first time, Demetria smiled. "Just follow the path at the end of the driveway. You can't miss it."

He almost did miss the path, and even though he was at the Villa Prospero and it was only a matter of minutes before he would see Philly, Roman found himself growing more and more anxious. Like the rabbit in *Alice in Wonderland,* he felt that he was late for a very important date. He didn't possess any of the Angelis psychic powers, but his instincts seldom failed him in business. Right now his gut was telling him that Philly was in some kind of trouble. Was he too late?

In spite of the rugged terrain, the question had him stepping up his pace. He nearly stumbled when he saw the white cat burst out of the woods and streak across his path.

Philly appeared next. There were pine needles in her hair and fear in her eyes. He barely had time to absorb those details before she crashed into him, threw her arms around him and held on for dear life.

At last. Roman threaded his fingers through her hair and pressed her close against him. For the first time since he'd landed on Corfu, he felt his anxiety ease. For a few seconds, there was only the sound of Philly's ragged breathing and the rustle of the wind in the trees. He'd never held her like this before, never felt that slender, firm body pressed to his. She fit perfectly.

"There's…a man," Philly said, her breath hitching.

"Did he hurt you?" Roman drew her away so that he could study her face. "Are you all right?"

"Yes. I'm…" Her breath hitched again. "…fine. He's on the beach. He's…"

"Shh," he murmured. She wasn't hurt, he told himself. Frightened, yes. Fury at whatever—or whoever—had scared her threatened to rise up, but he tamped it down. Something had happened on that beach, and as soon as she settled he'd get it out of her. Then he'd handle it. But for now, she was safe. She was here. For the first time he noticed that she'd cut her hair very short. The curls and even that straight sophisticated bob were gone. In the dappled light, filtering through the trees, she made him think of one of Shakespeare's more ethereal woodland creatures.

For a moment, neither of them spoke, but Roman felt the air around them grow thick and charged. Desire sprang from the same place the fury had a moment ago, and he couldn't block it. Or he didn't want to.

"Why are you here?" she asked.

For this. Unable to stop himself, Roman lowered his mouth to hers.

Her lips parted. In surprise? In acceptance? Roman couldn't be sure, but he didn't care. Kissing her was a mistake, and there would be consequences. But he'd waited forever to really taste her. Just this once, he told himself. But once her flavor flooded his mouth, he knew that was a lie. And he could have sworn that the rocky ground beneath his feet shifted.

She was sweeter than he'd imagined, but there was a bite beneath the sweetness. As he took the kiss deeper, he discovered a dark richness that he'd never experienced before. Then her scent wrapped around him and it wasn't sweet at all. It was exotic, erotic, and it made him think of the Sirens who'd lured sailors to their deaths. For the first time, Roman understood why they would have gone willingly.

At last. That was the only coherent thought that formed in my mind once Roman pressed his mouth to mine. I felt as if I'd come home. Then he nipped at my bottom lip, changed the angle of the kiss, and I felt as if I'd just entered a brave, new world.

The sound of the sea, so muted before, grew louder. The breeze so gentle just seconds ago whipped around us, a storm seemed to be brewing.

I could feel everything so acutely. One of my hands was trapped against his chest and his heart hammered frantically against my palm. His taste—I'd imagined it so often, but it was so…potent. His touch burned my skin and sent thrill after thrill rippling through me. But it was his mouth I craved more of. It was so tempting that I took and took and took.

Still, I wanted more. I strained closer. As if answering my demand, he slipped one hand between us and covered my breast. Pleasure so sharp that it bordered on pain arrowed through me.

His other hand gripped my hip and lifted. Wrapping arms and legs around him, I scooted up until we were pressed center to center, heat to heat. It still wasn't enough. I couldn't get close enough. My heart was beating so hard, so fast that I was surprised it didn't burst right out of me.

Then suddenly, abruptly, he set me down on the path. I cried out in protest, but he took a quick step back.

"No. I can't. We can't."

"What?" I gave my head a shake, trying to clear it. "What?"

"I'm sorry. I never should have—" He broke off to run a hand through his hair. The other one was clenched at his side.

Anger shot through me, and some of my brain cells clicked on. He was apologizing! Again! Suddenly I wasn't just mad, I was furious. "You never should have what? Followed me here to Greece? Looked at me as if you wanted to eat me whole? Kissed me?"

"It was a mistake."

This time it was pain that shot through me. But I pushed it away, fisted my hands on my hips and sent him a killing look. "A mistake?"

Roman said nothing. He was staring at me as if he was seeing me for the first time. But I was seeing red. Over the years, I'd worked on controlling my temper, but at times it slipped away from me. Usually right after I saw red.

I lunged at him and shoved him hard enough to make him fall on his butt. "What you are, Roman Oliver, is a big fat liar."

I wanted to jump him. I wanted to grab him by the shoulders and shake him until his head rattled. But if I went near him again, even for a moment, I was afraid that I would simply beg him to finish what he'd started.

I summoned up all the pride I could muster and pointed a finger at him instead. "Maybe you think it was a mistake to kiss me. Your loss. And you can stuff your apology. But don't you ever try to tell me that you think of me just as a sister."

I wanted to leave then. But my dramatic exit was impeded by the fact that Roman was blocking my path. His eyes never left mine as he rose and brushed off his pants. "Tell me about the man on the beach."

My anger drained away as all the terror and panic I'd felt ever since I'd seen the bullet send up that telltale spray of sand came flooding back. "He's dead." I glanced around, looking for Ariel, but there was no sign of her. And I couldn't feel her, either. I had to hope she'd headed for the Villa Prospero and safety.

Roman's eyes narrowed. "There's a dead man on the beach?"

I lifted my chin. "I'll show you." Then, whirling, I started through the woods, retracing the route that the cat and I had taken up the hill. So I was able to execute my dramatic exit after all.

TEN MINUTES LATER, I stood next to Roman on the white sand, exactly where the man in the wide-brimmed hat had been lying when Ariel had led me to him. Only he wasn't there. The red stain caused by his blood was gone, too. There wasn't even a depression in the sand where his body had been. Roman and I hadn't spoken on the climb down the hill—not even when I'd slipped and fallen and he'd helped me up— but as much as I hated to admit it, I was glad that he was here. I felt a lot less spooked than I would have otherwise.

"He's gone," I said, stating the all too obvious.

"You're sure this is the spot?"

Since it was a legitimate question and there was no trace of skepticism in his tone, I kept the annoyance out of mine. "I'm positive."

"Any chance that there's another little cove similar to this one and we angled down the wrong way?"

I'd already asked myself that question. I pointed at the Castello. "There's only one cove that's flanked by a fourteenth-century fortress."

Roman glanced up at the towers. "Good point. And the man was lying right here?"

I squatted. "His feet were about here, and he was medium height."

"Could you tell how he'd died?"

I drew in a deep breath as the image of the man's body filled my mind. "He had a bullet hole in the side of his head." I tapped a finger against my left temple. Then I pointed to the spot on the hillside where I'd seen the flash of light. "I think the killer shot from up there just below the Castello."

"You actually spotted him?"

I shook my head. "I just saw a flash of reflected sunlight when I was racing after Ariel."

Roman frowned. "Ariel?"

"The white cat."

"The same one I saw dash out of the woods just before I bumped into you?"

I nodded. "She was the one who led me to the body—she was very upset. I'm assuming because of the name that she belongs to my cousin Alexi. He has two cats and one of them, Caliban, is missing. I'm hoping that Ariel is back safe at the Villa Prospero."

Roman stared out at the sea, then walked in a wide circle around the area I'd indicated. "Can you tell if the tide's coming in?"

I glanced at the waves and noted that they were closer than they'd been before. The base of the boulder that one of the bullets had ricocheted off of was wet now. "It's coming in. That boulder was totally dry before." Then I saw light reflect off metal. Moving to the boulder, I leaned down and retrieved a cell phone. "It could be the victim's. He had one in his hand when I first saw him."

"That will help the police identify him," Roman said.

I tucked it into my pocket.

Roman studied the water. "How much time has passed since you first saw the body?"

I'd completely lost track of time since I'd realized I was being shot at, so I glanced at my watch, then considered briefly. It was nearly one-thirty and my driver dropped me off at noon. "A half hour to forty-five minutes."

"So the body couldn't have been carried off by the tide."

"No."

Turning, Roman met my eyes directly. I could read nothing in his expression, I had no way of telling whether he believed me or not. Even with the cell phone, I wasn't sure I would have believed myself.

Finally, he said, "The killer must have come back and cleaned up after himself."

Relief streamed through me. Then I glanced around. "Maybe not entirely." I rose and walked over to the spot where I'd seen the sand spurt up near the white cat. The image was indelibly imprinted on my mind. The sand was damp now. Squatting, I began to dig with my fingers. On the fifth scoop I found the bullet and held it up for Roman to see. "He missed this."

Roman's eyes narrowed as he strode toward me. "How did you know that was there?"

"He shot at the cat, too. One of them ricocheted off the rock. Then I saw the sand spurt up."

Roman glanced up at the Castello, then grabbed my

free hand and urged me toward the trees at the foot of the hill. Once we were in their shelter, he told me to sit down and then he sat down beside me. "Start at the beginning, Philly. And tell me everything."

4

By THE TIME we finally reached the Villa Prospero, my initial adrenaline rush at finding the body had faded, and I was beginning to react to the reality of the situation. Telling Roman what had happened had brought all the details vividly to my mind. Since we hadn't talked on the climb back up to the villa, I'd had time to dwell on them.

A man was dead. And someone had disposed of his body. A bone-deep chill moved through me, and I shivered.

Roman turned to me immediately and took my arm. "Are you all right?"

I nodded. "Just a bit of a delayed reaction, I think."

"You're going to have to repeat the whole thing to the police."

"I can do that." I squared my shoulders in reaction to the concern I heard in his voice. "I'm a big girl, Roman."

Miranda was at the registration desk and she looked up with a polite smile when we walked into the lobby. I noted again the combination of neatness and elegance in her appearance.

I knew from Aunt Cass and my father that Miranda was only in her early forties, but she looked even younger. She'd married early to Sandro Kostas, a man her parents had chosen for her so that she would have help running the hotel after they passed away. Kostas had left her a widow three years ago. Before his death, she'd spent most of her time seeing to the cuisine and keeping the books. Sandro had played the host. But it seemed to me as though Miranda was doing well as a hostess—she looked far more assured than she'd been earlier when Mr. Magellan had confronted her.

"Philly?" Her face brightened as she moved toward me and took both of my hands in hers. "Spiro's daughter. You're even prettier than your pictures. Welcome, welcome. It's such a pleasure to have you here. I'm so sorry I didn't greet you properly when you arrived. Demetria should have told me."

"Don't blame her—I told her not to. I wanted to walk on the beach and I ran into a white cat. Did she come back here?"

As she shook her head, a faint frown appeared on Miranda's forehead. "That might have been Ariel. But I haven't seen her at all today. She may have gone to look for my son, Alexi."

Miranda turned to Roman then. "Demetria told me that you know my cousin Philly?"

Roman smiled at her. "I know her very well. I'm her brother Kit Angelis." He held out a hand, and Miranda grasped it warmly, her face a mixture of surprise and delight.

I simply stood there and stared at him. Later, I would tell myself that my mental state had been approaching shock. That had to have been why I said nothing.

"Welcome! I was only expecting Philly. This is such a wonderful surprise—to have two of Spiro's children visit."

I'm sure my mouth was hanging open, but neither of them was paying me any heed. I felt as if I were watching a play.

Roman squeezed Miranda's hands. "You must forgive me for not calling ahead. But my plans changed at the last minute, and I wanted to surprise my sister. My father and

Helena so enjoyed their visit here and I can see why." He paused to glance around the room. "You have a lovely place."

I wanted to surprise my sister? Never in my life had I knowingly watched anyone lie so smoothly.

Miranda said something in reply, but I missed it because Roman chose that moment to meet my eyes. There was a challenge in his—almost as if he was daring me to expose his lie. I told myself I had to say something, to put a stop to his little masquerade before it went any further, but my lips just wouldn't form the words.

He shifted his gaze back to Miranda. "And you're not to worry. Demetria has already told me that you're completely booked, but I can bunk in with Philly. All I need is a cot."

"Of course you'll stay here," Miranda said. "And you won't need a cot. The sofa in the suite converts to a bed. As soon as my son returns, I'll have him make it up. In the meantime, you must go out to the terrace. I'll bring you coffee and pastries. We're through serving lunch, but I can have Demetria fix some sandwiches."

I finally had my mouth open to say something when Roman preempted me. "Before we sit down, we have to contact the police."

Miranda turned back at that, surprise and worry in her eyes. "The police?"

"Philly found a dead body on the beach."

"A dead body?"

Fear flashed into her eyes, and I sensed she might be worried about Alexi. "A man—medium height and stocky. He was wearing a wide-brimmed hat—like the ones you sell in your gift shop—and he was carrying a backpack and binoculars."

"Does he sound familiar?" Roman asked.

Miranda frowned thoughtfully, then shook her head.

"There are so many visitors on the island right now because of the party at the Castello Corli the day after tomorrow. Andre Magellan throws these parties at least twice a year. His guests number in the hundreds. He can accommodate most of them at the Castello—it's reputed to have close to one hundred guest rooms—but we take the overflow here." She shifted her gaze to Roman. "How did the man die?"

"We believe he was shot by someone up on the cliff near the Castello," Roman explained. "Philly was on her way back here when she ran into me. By the time we returned to the beach, the body was gone."

"Gone?"

"The killer may not have wanted it found," Roman explained.

"When I first spotted the man, there was someone with him—a younger man he seemed to be arguing with," I said. "He was about the same height with dark curly hair. My guess is that he's still in his teens, and he was wearing some kind of medal around his neck."

Miranda shook her head, but I didn't miss the slight stiffening of her body. My description had made her think of someone, I was sure of it.

"That was where I first saw the white cat," I said. "She led me to the body."

"Ariel," Miranda breathed and then clasped her hands together. "It must have been Ariel. Her twin brother, Caliban, has been missing for two days. Alexi has been very upset. He and those cats have been inseparable since his father gave them to him. He's spent the last two days searching along the coastline." Dropping her hands to her sides, she gave us a flustered glance. "Please forgive me for rambling on. Come out to the terrace. You'll have something to drink while I call the police."

Miranda seated us at a table in the shade of some pines and poured us each a glass of pale gold wine before she hurried back to the lobby.

The moment she was out of earshot, Roman said, "Take a sip of that. You're still looking a little shaky. I have to make a couple of calls."

I didn't argue. I was barely able to keep my hand from trembling as I lifted the glass. The wine was cool, but it helped to take the edge off of the chill that was settling over me.

Demetria appeared and set a pot of coffee and a tray of pastries on the table. I smiled and nodded my thanks and then returned my gaze to Roman. He was talking on his cell to a man he called Gianni. Or rather listening. The man on the other end seemed to be doing most of the talking. From what I could gather, they were discussing something about hotels.

Sitting there in the dappled sunlight, Roman was at his ease, the picture of self-containment and confidence. Having him here was helping. This man seated across from me was the Roman I was familiar with—cool, competent.

"I'll be delayed longer than I originally thought," Roman said. "A day or two."

The man who'd told Miranda that he was my brother Kit was a bit of a stranger. So was the man who'd kissed me on the hillside path. There'd been nothing cool about that kiss. I'd tasted a desperation that had matched my own. These new aspects of Roman intrigued me.

At the same time his ability to return to normal mode so quickly annoyed me. He was calmly conducting business while my mind was still spinning. I wasn't even at the point where I could sort out my thoughts.

And I couldn't blame it totally on a delayed reaction to finding a dead man on the beach.

I tried to focus by concentrating on one thing. There was the cat, Ariel. I'd sensed a bone-deep, almost frantic, fear in her. Ariel had reminded me a bit of Pretzels, and I wondered if it was part of her nature to react in a very dramatic way. Not that she didn't have a perfect right to be afraid. It was very possible that she'd seen a man get shot. But she'd been distressed even when the man in the wide-brimmed hat was still alive.

Worry and concern about her brother may very well have been the source of the chaotic emotions I'd first sensed in Ariel. I recalled the image of the white cat lying in darkness. Could that have been Caliban? The picture hadn't been clear, but it did look as though he was alive and he had a supply of food and water. I wished that Ariel hadn't disappeared when I'd kissed Roman on the path.

I'd been trying to avoid thinking about that kiss. As lust curled snakelike in my stomach, I reached for my wine and took a long swallow. For a moment I sat there simply studying Roman. He was seated with his back to the marvelous view of the sea beyond. He'd angled his chair slightly so that he wasn't facing me, and that meant he didn't notice that I was staring.

I thought of how often I'd dreamed of kissing him. The first fantasies had been the innocent ones of a sixteen-year-old, but as I'd entered college and gained some experience with men, my fantasies had become more detailed. Still, nothing, actual or imagined, had prepared me for the reality of Roman's callused palms or his clever, demanding mouth. I'd never before felt my will drain so completely away. He could have asked anything of me, and I would have given it. Gladly.

Another moment and we would have made love right there on the path. But he'd pulled away. And then he'd had the nerve to apologize. Again. The anger I'd felt earlier came surging back. I started to sip my wine once more, then decided on coffee instead. I needed to keep a clear head if I was going to deal with the man sitting across from me. And I was going to have to figure out how to deal with him since he'd clearly decided to hang around for the next day or two.

The coffee was strong and bitter, just the way my father brewed it at his restaurant, and it immediately began to counteract the wine I'd had. I decided the question I most needed the answer to was why Roman had told Miranda that he was Kit. Had it been to emphasize to me that he thought of me only as a brother?

I narrowed my eyes on him. Fat chance he was going to get away with that story twice. I was beginning to think that I'd been a fool to believe it the first time he'd told it.

Demetria stepped out onto the terrace and hurried toward our table. "Mrs. Kostas sends her apologies. She's busy with some of the other guests. She said to tell you that Inspector Ionescu is on his way. Can I get you anything else?"

I smiled at her, assured her that we were fine, and she hurried away again. Through the open doors of the terrace, I could see several guests lined up to talk to Miranda. At least two of the men were wearing hats similar to the one I'd seen on the dead man.

I turned my gaze back to Roman. Maybe I was asking the wrong question. What did it matter why Roman had lied to Miranda? The question I ought to be asking was what was *I* going to do about the fact that Roman and I were going to be sharing a room?

Roman closed his cell and turned his chair so that he was facing me. "Your cousin lied to us about not knowing the younger man on the beach."

He was definitely in normal mode, I thought. I quickly gathered my thoughts so that I would appear to be also. "Yes, I agree. I think it might have been Alexi I saw. And she was worried at first that he might be the dead man. Alexi must be in some kind of trouble." I told Roman about my initial arrival at the Villa Prospero and the scene I'd witnessed between Miranda and Andre Magellan.

Roman poured himself a cup of coffee. "How old is Alexi?"

"Eighteen. According to my father and Helena, he was always a little behind in school. Not retarded, but a little slow developmentally."

"That might explain his single-minded determination to find his missing cat and the way he's ignoring Magellan's warnings and neglecting his duties here."

I lifted my chin. "I can understand his concern. If Pretzels or Peanuts were missing, I might neglect a few of my duties also."

"Point taken. What else can you tell me about Alexi?"

"Dad told me that since Miranda's husband died three years ago, she's depended on Alexi to help her run the place."

"He would have been fifteen. That's a lot of responsibility for a young man." Roman sipped coffee and leaned back in his chair. "I was a little older than that when I started to take an active role at Oliver Enterprises. After my mother died, my dad…well, he wasn't himself for a while. I had to take on more responsibility in the company—more than he would have given me under other circumstances."

"You handled it." I couldn't imagine Roman not being able to handle anything.

His lips curved slightly. "Actually, I loved it. Working at Oliver Enterprises, expanding our business has always been my goal. So much so that I didn't want to go to college. My dad insisted. Good thing or I never would have ended up being Kit's roommate." He sipped more coffee. "Alexi may not be as enthusiastic about running this hotel. Miranda must have asked him not to hang around the Castello. He may be acting out a bit in rebellion."

I studied him. It occurred to me that Roman and I had never sat like this before—just the two of us talking. Thinking about it, I realized that we'd always been with my family or his—except for those two times in his hospital room. It was at that moment that I caught a glimpse of that white bird again spiraling upward in the blue sky above the sea. The same feelings I'd experienced on the cliff path moved through me. And I knew—the same way that I often sensed things with animals—that this was where I was meant to be and that Roman was meant to be here with me. Whatever adventure lay ahead of me on this island, Roman was fated to be a part of it.

"There's another problem." Roman paused, then said, "Philly?"

"Sorry." I gathered my thoughts and met his eyes. "You were saying there's a problem."

"Inspector Ionescu may have some trouble investigating a murder with no body. The only evidence we have to show him is that shell casing. The cell phone will help with identification, but it doesn't prove a homicide."

"I know what I saw."

"And I believe you." Roman topped off the coffee in our cups. "But I'm trying to look at the situation from your brother Nik's point of view."

I saw where he was going. Nik would see everything through a cop's skeptical eyes.

"There's very little for the police to work with. If you

wanted to tell them that you think it might have been your cousin arguing with the man just before he was shot, Alexi could at least corroborate your story about seeing them on the beach."

"I don't want to say that yet. I can't be positive that it was Alexi. I've never even met him."

"Are you worried that Alexi could be the shooter?" Roman asked.

"No." I shook my head vehemently. "The man arguing with the victim wouldn't have had time to get all the way up the cliff to where I think the shooter was."

"Good point." Roman sipped more coffee, studying me over the rim of his cup.

"It's too bad that Inspector Ionescu can't question Ariel."

Roman's brows shot up. "The cat?"

I nodded. "She may have witnessed the murder."

"Could you question her?"

I glanced around. "I'd like to. I'm worried about her. The sniper shot twice at her."

"Do you think she can tell you who he is?"

I studied him for a moment. It occurred to me that he'd not once questioned anything I'd told him about my communication with Ariel. He seemed to accept my ability to connect with animals with the same ease that my family did. "I don't know if she saw who it was. If the killing shot came from where the other shots came from, the shooter was too far up the cliff side."

"But he may have been closer to the beach when he fired that shot."

I frowned. Neither of us said anything, but that possibility meant that the man we were beginning to believe was Alexi could have shot the older man.

"I'll ask her the next time I see her."

"Just how do you do it—communicate with animals, I mean?"

"You're very accepting of my ability."

"I've listened to Kit brag about you for years. But he's never shared the specifics of how it works. Do they talk to you?"

"Sometimes I hear actual words in my head. But other times it's all images and sometimes colors. With Ariel, I saw red." I clasped my hands tightly in front of me. "It was all that blood on the white sand." When I'd described what had happened to Roman, I'd summarized my communication with Ariel, but I'd left out most of the specifics. "When I first saw her through my camera lens, I sensed emotions—fear, frustration and a huge sense of urgency. She wanted something and she wasn't about to be soothed. After the younger man leaned over to pet her, she backed away."

"Isn't it odd that she would back away if the younger man was Alexi?"

I thought about it for a moment. Once again talking to Roman was helping me to clarify everything. "She wanted something—help, I think. That was the first thing she said to me when she appeared around the rocks. When I found the body, I assumed she wanted help for him. But I think she was looking for help even before the man in the hat was shot. That's why she wouldn't let the younger man pet her for long. She was on a mission."

"Any ideas about why she ran toward you for help after the man in the hat was killed?"

I hadn't considered that. "When I first felt a connection with her, the feelings were so intense. Perhaps she sensed me, too. She also sent me an image. I didn't mention it earlier because it didn't seem to be connected to the murder. I saw a white cat lying motionless in a dark place."

"Her brother?"

"That's what I'm wondering. I have a lot of questions that I think she could answer. And I have a few for Alexi, too."

"You're not going to keep out of this, are you?"

I leaned toward him. "How can I? I found that body on the beach. And Ariel asked for help. When she comes back I want to try and find a way to help her."

Roman was about to say something else, but I held up a hand to stop him. "Look, if you're going to try to persuade me to leave, you're wasting your time. From the moment I stepped out of the taxi, I've been certain that I'm meant to be here."

"Fate?"

"Yes."

"Why are you so sure of that?"

It wasn't skepticism I heard in his voice. If it had been, I probably would have kept my mouth shut. But the thing I was discovering about Roman was that he was a patient listener, down on the beach and again right now. He was an easy man to talk to. And sometimes truth was the most effective weapon.

Aunt Cass was always saying that the Fates only offered a choice. It was always up to the person to grab on to what was offered.

"I'm sure that Kit has told you that my family has a history of finding their soul mates here in Greece—first my mother and Aunt Cass and most recently my dad. So after you turned down my proposition at the hospital, I decided that I'd try my luck over here. Not that I'm looking for my true love—exactly. I'd settle for a really hot fling. But life is nothing if not ironic. Instead of finding a lover on the beach, I found a dead man."

When Roman said nothing, I hurried on. "I'm convinced

he's just the beginning of the adventure. I know that the Fates have brought me here, and I'm not going to leave until I find out all that they have in store for me."

There was a sort of nonplussed expression on Roman's face that I'd never seen before. It gave me the courage to say, "Now that I've bared my soul to you, turnabout's fair play. Why did you lie to Miranda and tell her you were Kit?"

I WISH THE HELL I KNEW. Roman had been pondering that very question ever since the lie had slipped so easily out of his mouth. He knew how to guard his tongue. He'd cultivated the skill in countless business negotiations. Still, he'd told Miranda he was Kit without missing a beat.

Why?

The surface answer was easy enough. "I'd already heard from Demetria that they had no rooms available. She offered to get me a room in the nearest village. There's no way I'm leaving you here alone until this matter is sorted out."

Her chin lifted in just the way he'd known it would. "I don't need a big brother. I can handle myself."

"You weren't doing so well when I ran into you on the cliff path."

"That was only because you were there. If you hadn't been, I would have been fine."

Roman didn't doubt that for a moment. Still he was glad that he'd been there. He thought of what she'd looked like right after he'd apologized for kissing her and she'd knocked him flat on his ass. She'd reminded him of Aphrodite—beautiful, powerful and furious. A goddess you wouldn't want to mess with. And he'd wanted her mindlessly. God help him, he still did.

And that was the other reason he'd lied to Miranda.

But what he said was, "You believe the sniper was

shooting at the cat. Who's to say his next shot wouldn't have been aimed at you?"

She swallowed hard. "He missed the cat. Twice. Maybe he was just trying to scare us away so he could get rid of the body."

Roman nodded. "That's possible. But once we report all this to the inspector, and the shooter finds out you're still here at the villa—not only here, but asking questions—he might decide you saw too much."

"If you're trying to frighten me—"

"I am."

"I'm not leaving."

"Neither am I."

There was a beat. Then Philly leaned forward and there was a glint in her eye he couldn't recall seeing before. "Fine. But if we're going to share the same room, I want to lay down some ground rules."

"Ground rules?" What in hell was coming next?

"You're a businessperson. You must be familiar with the concept." She lifted her wineglass and sipped. "The next time you kiss me—no pulling back, no apologies. You'd better be prepared to finish what you start."

The challenge was clear in her voice, in her eyes. But he was saved from a direct reply when Miranda ushered a thin, wiry man of medium height and sharp, intelligent eyes onto the terrace.

"Philly, Kit, this is Inspector Ionescu," Miranda said. "Inspector, these are my cousins from San Francisco."

5

DURING THE TWO HOURS Roman and I had spent in the company of Inspector Ionescu, I'd learned he was a very professional and thorough man. I'm embarrassed to admit that I'd expected someone who was a bit more of a hick—or at the least someone more rumpled or cranky. The inspector was none of the above.

He sat across a table from me in a shaded and isolated part of the terrace flipping through a small notebook. The first word that had popped into my mind from the moment I'd seen him was *dapper*. He reminded me a bit of the actor who'd starred as Agatha Christie's Hercule Poirot in the British television series. His build was thin and wiry. He wore neatly pressed khaki trousers, a short-sleeved shirt and tie and sturdy boots that had served him well when he'd accompanied Roman and me to the crescent-shaped beach where I'd last seen the body. I was hoping that I might catch a glimpse of Ariel on the way down, but I hadn't.

Before we'd climbed down the cliff path, Ionescu had questioned Roman and me separately in Miranda's office. Once we returned to the villa, he'd separated us again. Roman now sat several tables away, sipping coffee and chatting with Demetria.

Ionescu closed his notebook and glanced up at me. "Is there anything else you can tell me, Ms. Angelis?"

I pretended to think for a moment, and then I said, "No."

Ionescu said nothing. Out of the corner of my eye, I could see that Roman was perfectly at his ease while my stomach was knotted with nerves. I'd been lying to the inspector for two hours.

"You don't have any idea of the identity of the young man you saw talking with the victim?"

"No."

He was looking right into my eyes, and I prayed that he couldn't read my mind. Because I did have an idea of who the younger man was. Still, I didn't know for sure that it had been my cousin Alexi.

"Is there anything about what you've told me that you'd like to change?"

"No." That was a lie also. Because I wanted very badly to tell him that Roman wasn't my brother Kit. Roman and I had argued about that point on the beach while Ionescu had been some distance away searching the promontory of rocks near the Castello. I'd pointed out that the inspector was going to discover that Roman was lying anyway. He was definitely going to check our passports. Or he could privately Google Kit's name if he didn't want us to know he was curious about us. My brother Kit had two different Web sites—one for his P.I. business and the other for his novels. His picture was prominently displayed on both. All Roman had said was that he'd handle that when the time came.

Somehow I didn't think Ionescu was going to approve of Roman's timing.

When Ionescu slipped the small notebook into his pocket and rose, Roman walked to the table to join us. "All finished, Inspector?"

"For the moment. Have you thought of anything else I should know, Mr. Angelis?"

"No—I believe we've covered it all. What will you do next?"

"I'll trace the owner of the cell phone Ms. Angelis found. Then we'll have a name. Whether or not it belongs to the victim is another question. By tomorrow, I may have a report of a missing person, either from here or the Castello Corli. I'd like the two of you to keep yourselves available." He handed Roman his card. "And if you think of anything else I need to know, please call me at once."

After nodding at me, Ionescu moved toward the lobby. Roman and I watched him stop and speak to Miranda. To my surprise, he reached out and touched her arm in a gesture that spoke of comfort.

I murmured to Roman, "They know each other more than professionally."

"If that's true, then he knows Alexi also."

"And probably recognized him from the description I gave of the younger man on the beach." I rose from the table. "I'm worried about Ariel and Caliban."

"I spoke to Demetria about the cats. She says that ever since Caliban went missing, Ariel disappears for long periods of time. She may be with Alexi."

I thought of the image of the white cat lying in the shadowy place. He was awake, just not moving. Maybe he couldn't. "Perhaps she goes to her brother. That would make sense especially if she's a worrier like my Pretzels is." I recalled the remains of the small animal. "She may be bringing him food. And I saw water."

"There's nothing you can do right now. Not until Ariel returns."

When I glanced over my shoulder, I saw that Ionescu was still talking to Miranda. "The inspector suspects we're lying about something. You should have told him you're not Kit."

"Miranda wouldn't approve of my staying in your room if she learned the truth right now. I'm sure she feels that while you're at the Villa Prospero, she's standing in for your father. I wouldn't want to add to the stress she's under by insisting that I stay in your room as Roman Oliver."

I met his eyes steadily. "I'm a grown woman. I make my own decisions about who stays or does not stay in my room."

Though his expression didn't change I could tell he was amused. "That doesn't alter the way your brothers would feel if they knew we were sharing a room. I know what I'd feel about my sisters."

My brows shot up. "Theo is sharing a room with your sister Sadie on a pretty regular basis."

"That's different. There's a commitment between Theo and Sadie." All trace of amusement disappeared from his eyes. "I'm not a man who can make that kind of commitment, Philly. Running Oliver Enterprises is much more than a full-time job to me. It's something I've worked for all of my life. I've watched my father try to juggle the responsibilities of business and family and now he's heading for his third divorce. I decided some time ago that it wouldn't be fair to ask someone to share my life when I would have so little time to devote to the relationship."

With my temper surging, I closed the distance between us and poked a finger into his chest. "Let's clear something up right now. I've never mentioned the C *or* the M word. I told you in your hospital room exactly what I wanted. I want to make love with you. Period." Warming to my theme, I poked him again. "For two cents—"

Just in time, I reined in my anger and clamped my teeth together. I'd nearly threatened to expose his identity to Miranda and insist that she find him a room in the village. Thank heavens my more rational side prevailed. Because I didn't want Roman staying someplace in the village. I wanted him in my room tonight. I was going to take what the Fates were offering me. I was going to take Roman Oliver.

Roman was looking at me as if he was seeing something he hadn't seen before. "For two cents, you'd what?" he asked.

"Knock you on your ass again," I said.

He chuckled then, and the sound had the rest of my temper draining away.

"C'mon." He took my arm and led me toward the lobby. "Demetria said that our room is ready, and we'll want to freshen up. Drinks are served at seven, dinner at eight."

It was almost six. I figured that would give me plenty of time to implement stage one of my plan.

HANDLING PHILLY was going to be a problem. Roman knew it in the same gut way that he always knew when a business deal threatened to go south. He stood on the small balcony that opened off the living room of Philly's suite. The rooms were small but well appointed, and the view of the sea below was one of the best that the villa had to offer. The sun was lowering in the sky and the scent of lemons filled the air.

But it was Philly's scent that lingered in his mind. It had been haunting him ever since he'd kissed her. She'd used the shower first, so when it was his turn, each breath he'd inhaled had filled his mind with images of how it might feel to have her standing in the shower with him. He'd imagined running his hands over that slender body that he'd just begun to explore on the cliff path. Of molding her slick with soap against him. Hardness to softness. Heat to heat.

Spinning the fantasy out in his head, he'd lifted her and once she'd wrapped her legs around him, he'd pressed her against the wall and entered her slowly, drawing out the pleasure for them both until her wet heat totally engulfed him.

He'd very nearly come just thinking about it.

Turning, he glanced at the closed door to the bedroom. She'd been throwing him one curveball after another ever since she'd walked into his hospital room and propositioned him. And he could admit now that it had been a mistake to follow her here—the result of acting on impulse—something he rarely did. And now he felt trapped. How could he leave her? She was in trouble, and so, however distant the connection might be, was her family.

Someone had been murdered. Ionescu was a good man, competent. But there was no way to tell how successful the investigation would be or how long it would take. In the meantime, Philly had planted herself firmly in the middle of whatever was going on. If the young man she'd seen arguing with the dead man turned out to be her cousin, Ionescu would have a lot of questions for him. Then there were the cats.

Though he'd done his best to calm her worries about them earlier, there was no way she'd butt out until she was sure that both of them were safe. There was no way she'd butt out, period. The one thing he'd noticed about Philly was that once she set her sights on a goal, she always achieved it. Since she'd finished her degree in psychology, she'd slowly but surely built up her pet-psychic business while juggling part-time jobs at a veterinary hospital and filling in as hostess at her family's restaurant. Kit bragged to him about each new client she got.

He glanced at his watch—a little after seven. She'd been getting dressed for over half an hour. He turned his attention back to the view. While Philly had been talking to Ionescu, Demetria had filled him in on the local legend that there was a kind of magic on the island that people could tap into. What you wished for could come true.

Standing on the balcony and watching the sun lower in the sky, Roman could almost believe the legend was real. Demetria's English was more enthusiastic than clear, but from what he'd pieced together it was based on the belief held by many that Corfu had been the inspiration for the setting of Shakespeare's *The Tempest*. Perhaps some of Prospero's magic still lingered and that was why he was feeling so bewitched.

Philly had made it pretty clear what she'd come to the island wishing for. Sex with a stranger. Recalling how she'd talked so casually of making love with some man she hadn't even met yet, jealousy once again sliced through Roman with the precision of a surgeon's scalpel. He was getting tired of the sensation and damn tired of wanting someone he'd told himself he couldn't have.

He turned when the door opened and watched Philly step into the room. For a moment, he couldn't breathe and his mind emptied. The one stray thought that tumbled into the void was that this wasn't the Philly he'd known for years. Either it was the new haircut or she'd done something to her eyes that made them look larger. And her lips were a siren red. But it was the dress—or the lack of it— that had his throat going dry. The silky material that dropped from thin straps at her shoulders to stop well above her knees and hugged every curve of her body.

He had to work to keep from staring at her legs. Then she turned around and he gave up the battle. The dress was backless, and the combination of white skin and black dress had him thinking of magic again.

"What do you think?" she asked. "The saleslady guaranteed this dress was male bait."

His only thought was that he would have to fight each and every one of those men off.

"Well?" Philly prodded, turning in another circle. As she did, the dress flared and revealed more leg.

"The saleswoman was right." Roman was surprised that he'd actually formed words. "Shall we?" He gestured toward the door and gave her a wide berth as he led the way. If he stayed in this room one second longer, the fantasy he'd indulged in earlier during his shower would become a reality. Once in the hall, he drew in a deep breath and stifled an impulse to run. As they made their way down the hall, he hoped that the drinks on the terrace would include something much stronger than wine.

"I THINK THIS PLACE is a magical spot, don't you?" Roman and I were seated on the terrace, lingering over a final glass of wine and some pastries. The sun was sinking into the sea and the sky was streaked with shades of blue and rose.

"The cuisine certainly is," Roman said.

I was sure that the food was excellent, but I'd hardly tasted any of it. Our conversation had passed the time pleasantly enough. We'd avoided the topics of the dead man and the sniper and my still-missing cousin Alexi. And talking to Roman earlier about the cats had eased my mind—I was convinced that Ariel was with her brother just as Pretzels would be with Peanuts if she were injured and in need of help.

Instead Roman and I had talked about our work. I'd learned that he was on his way to Athens where he was negotiating a deal with a Greek millionaire and entrepreneur, Gianni Stassis, to buy into select privately owned hotels in Greece. The Villa Prospero was a prime example of the type of place they would approach with their offer.

My contribution to the dinner conversation had been to describe some of the more eccentric animals and owners that I worked with. But all the time what I really wanted was dessert, and he was sitting directly across from me.

Nerves jittered in my stomach, but I was determined to overcome them. I was just not going to let myself waste this opportunity. I ran my finger around the top of my wine-glass, just the way I'd seen Linda Hamilton do it in a made-for-TV movie called *Sex & Mrs. X.* After dipping my finger into the glass, I raised it to my mouth and licked the wine off. In the film, Linda was a journalist who was writing a story on the most famous madam in Paris, and she'd picked up several tricks on how to attract and seduce a man. This particular one seemed to be working on Roman.

Sexy seductress was not my usual role, but I was beginning to think that I might have a knack for it. The dress was helping. I'd never before worn anything quite like it, and the look right now in Roman's eyes was anything but brotherly. However, the man seemed to have a talent for running hot one minute and cold the next. Prime example—the kiss on the cliff path. I was still annoyed with him for pulling back.

Tonight, I wasn't about to leave anything up to chance. Roman Oliver was a businessman, so I'd decided that it might be a good idea to offer him a deal.

Leaning forward, I said, "I've been thinking. As I told you earlier, I came here to Greece to have a fling. But I haven't changed my mind about wanting to make love with you."

He didn't reply, but the look in his eyes could have liquefied my bones.

"Clearly, your story about your feelings for me being brotherly—well, that was an out-and-out lie. The way you kissed me on the cliff path wasn't brotherly."

He didn't deny it. In fact, he didn't say anything at all. Encouraged, I took a sip of wine and went on. "It occurred to me at some point during our individual sessions with Inspector Ionescu that any reservations you might have about having a sexual relationship with me because of my family don't apply here."

His eyes narrowed then. "They sure as hell do."

I raised a hand, palm out. "On the contrary. My father and brothers are back in San Francisco. We're thousands of miles away on a magical Greek island. They'll never have to know. And you've told my cousin that you're my brother. So all we have to do is be discreet in public."

"Philly—"

I ran a finger down the back of his hand (another *Sex & Mrs. X* tip). Not only did the gesture shut him up, but he turned his hand over and gripped mine. My throat went dry, and I felt the heat streak right to my center. Roman Oliver was going to be some dessert all right.

"You're a businessman, so I'm going to make you a deal. We'll have an affair, but it will only last as long as we're here on Corfu. And it will remain our secret. No one ever has to know. When we meet again in San Francisco, we'll go back to our old relationship—big brother, little sister."

He still said nothing. He merely looked at me. But the hunger in his eyes had my toes curling. I debated. I could just stand and take him with me to the room. But I wanted to nail down the deal first.

"Why don't we pretend we're strangers? We've just met for the first time tonight. I want you and you want me, and for the time we're here at the Villa Prospero, we'll enjoy each other. No strings. And no holds barred. Deal?"

There were three beats of silence and each one seemed like a mini-eternity. Finally Roman released my hand and rose. "I want to kiss you, and we can't do that here."

I couldn't feel my legs as we started back to the room.

"I hope that you don't regret this, Philly."

I wasn't sure about the regrets part, but I would worry about that later. What I had to concentrate on now was making sure that Roman would never forget me.

6

ONCE INSIDE THE ROOM, Roman moved fast, using his hands and body to trap me against the door. He threaded his fingers through my hair, then merely studied me. The light was dimming, but I had no trouble seeing his eyes. The heat had my breath catching, my body trembling.

He slid his hands to my shoulders, then down my arms. Flames licked along my nerve endings.

"Second thoughts?"

"No." Saying the word aloud only heightened my certainty that this was what I wanted. He was what I wanted. The need that had been building inside of me all through dinner was bordering on pain. "Touch me."

Settling his hands at my hips, he moved in closer. "I've been waiting all evening to do this." He traced a finger up my spine. I trembled. Then he spread his palms against my bare back and slowly ran them down to my waist. Fire shot through my veins. His eyes stayed on mine as he moved his hands again, faster this time, sliding up my sides until his palms pressed against the sides of my breasts. I was throbbing at every point a pulse could beat.

"Last chance, Philly." His voice had roughened. He was trying to be a gentleman, but I wasn't in the mood for one tonight.

"I'm not Philly, and you're not Roman, remember?"

I locked my arms around his neck and dragged his mouth to mine. It was hard and hot and I tasted barely leashed hunger. The flavor was so unique that I had to have more. His tongue took possession of my mouth, his teeth scraped my bottom lip, and the kiss teetered toward pain. And all the while those clever hands raced over me, tracing the curve of my throat, cupping my breasts, digging into my hips. The speed had my head spinning. Sensations swamped me as he lowered the zipper on the back of my dress and stripped me out of it.

I struggled with the buttons on his shirt. The sound of one dropping to the floor only made me more desperate. Finally, I ran my hands up that damp smooth skin, absorbing the hard ridge of muscles on his back.

He nipped at my bottom lip, then deepened the kiss until I felt as if I were drowning—sinking fast into someplace where the air was too thick to breathe. Wild fists of need battered at me, and the heat building inside me grew brutal. There was only one answer. I dragged my mouth from his. "Now. Right now."

I cried out in protest when he set me against the door and stepped away. But then he took his gaze on a searing journey over my body. He'd never looked at me that way before, and every muscle in me quivered with fresh delight. When he met my eyes again, I saw a simmering violence. Still, it wasn't fear or even apprehension I felt. It was a wild, hot thrill.

HE HAD TO GET a grip. Catch his breath. Think. This was Philly. She deserved gentleness, seduction. That had been his intention, but it had evaporated the instant she'd exploded in his arms. Even now that he wasn't touching her, tasting her, he couldn't get his head clear. The experience was unprecedented.

He prided himself on being a gentle, considerate lover, and he'd been about to mindlessly pound himself into her against a door. He still wanted to.

Stepping away from her wasn't doing a damn thing to cool his blood. The dress had been bewitching enough, but what she was wearing under it was designed to bring a man to his knees. All Roman could do was stare. Hopefully, his mouth hadn't dropped open and his tongue wasn't hanging out.

He was going to have to turn and walk away if he wanted to regain control. But he didn't move. He couldn't—any more than he could prevent himself from reaching out to run a finger over the black lace that topped one thigh-high stocking.

Meeting her eyes, Roman watched them darken as he trailed a finger up to the hint of a thong that barely covered her. Never would he have imagined Philly wearing anything like this. As he lingered there, barely touching her, the sound of her breathing—or was it his own?—grew ragged.

"Very nice." Still using a featherlight touch and keeping his gaze locked on hers, he moved his finger over her abdomen and up her midriff to hook it beneath the swatch of lace that barely covered her breasts. She was trembling now, and those brown eyes had misted over. He could see his own image reflected there and knew that she thought only of him.

Triumph raced through him along with a ferocious surge of need. To hell with seduction. He had to have her. The whispery sound of lace ripping only added fuel to the flash fire threatening to consume him. Lifting her, he took his mouth on a desperate journey from her breasts down the path his finger had traced. Her skin was damp, hot, her flavor so…necessary. But there was no time to savor, not when his blood pounded with such overwhelming greed.

Lace tore again as he straightened and pressed her back against the wall. Then he found her center and pierced her with two fingers.

Here was a heat that matched his own. He felt her inner muscles tighten around his fingers and watched her eyelids lower.

"No," he said. "Look at me when I make you come."

Then he absorbed each separate sensation—each tremor, each hitch of her breath as he shot her up, watched her ride the crest and shudder down. Her eyes blurred and went glassy. His name was a whispered moan that sent a fresh wave of heat slamming into him. He nearly came right then.

"Again." He didn't know who said the word as her fingers tore at his belt.

"This time…I want you inside me."

"Yes…" He wasn't sure he could survive another ten seconds if he wasn't inside of her. With whatever thin grip he had on his control, Roman managed to retrieve a condom from his pocket before his pants and belt hit the floor.

Her arms locked around his neck, her teeth sank into his shoulder. Then she whispered into his ear, "Make me come again."

Roman's head reeled.

"Protection," he said in a desperate attempt to keep his focus. His fingers shook as he sheathed himself.

"You'd better hurry." She nipped his earlobe, then pulled his mouth to hers. "I want you now."

"Right now." Gripping her hips, he hitched her up and drove into her where they stood. The door slammed hard into the jamb, and he was certain he heard his control snap in the same instant. Then her taste exploded inside of him, and he knew that he might never get enough. Of it. Of her.

His body took over, moving faster and faster. Hers kept pace, meeting him thrust for thrust until he knew nothing else, wanted nothing else but Philly. When she tightened around him like a slick, hot fist, he lost himself in her.

WHEN MY BRAIN CELLS clicked on again, I was straddling Roman's lap, my head on his shoulder. Bright moonlight streamed through the open balcony door. I had no idea how long we'd been sitting there like that. But I didn't want to move. Gradually, more details filtered through the sensual fog that still held me in its grip. I could see Roman's slacks pooled on the floor beside us. His back was against the door, his arms were around me…and he was still inside of me.

As my brain alerted my body to that fact, I felt my inner muscles tighten around him. Incredibly, fresh desire rippled through me.

He slipped a finger under my chin and drew my face up until our eyes met. I read concern in his.

"Are you all right, Philly?"

I smiled at him. "I keep telling you I'm not Philly." And I didn't feel like Philly anymore. It was as if my decision to seduce Roman and then finally making love with him had changed me. "But I *am* fabulous."

His gaze remained intent on mine. "You're sure I didn't hurt you?"

"Positive." I trailed a finger down his throat to his shoulder. "But I left teeth marks on you."

He smiled then. "Feel free—anytime."

Maybe it was the fact that he'd never smiled at me in quite that way before—a mixture of friendliness and intimacy. Or perhaps it was because he moved his hand until his fingers were spread against my cheek—but something stirred in me then. A knowledge, a certainty that I usually only experienced when I was communicating with animals.

This is the one.

An alarm sounded at the back of my mind. How often had Aunt Cass used just those words to describe what she'd felt, what she'd known the first time she'd seen my uncle Demetrius?

No. Roman Oliver wasn't *the one*. Panic bubbled in my stomach. That was something the old Philly had dreamed of for seven long years. I was not about to fall into that trap again. Roman and I were going to have a torrid affair, and I was going to get him out of my system. When we returned to San Francisco, we were going to go our separate ways. No harm, no foul.

More than that, I wasn't going to waste a moment of our time on Corfu worrying about silly childhood fantasies. Not when I could spend the time having incredible sex with Roman.

I traced my fingers over the bite mark. Then I lowered my mouth and bit him in the exact spot on his other shoulder. I felt him harden inside of me.

"Philly." He gripped my waist to lift me, but I clamped my legs on his thighs as I nibbled my way to his neck.

"You told me to feel free."

His fingers flexed at my waist. "If you keep that up, my plan to seduce you is going to be postponed again."

"Speaking totally for myself, I think your first plan worked out fine."

The laugh that vibrated from his throat sent a quick shiver through me. Straightening, I met his eyes. "I think it's my turn to seduce you. Only there's a rule. You can't touch me until I tell you to."

He raised his brows at that.

Since he was still wearing his shirt, I pushed it off his shoulders and down his arms, trapping them. "No cheating."

I bit into his lower lip, and his shudder had new flames igniting inside of me. Unable to resist, I crushed his mouth with mine, and my tongue tangled with his. This time, I had control of the kiss, and I tried to take my time, savoring his dark rich flavor.

But I wanted more—my body craved more—so I lifted my hips and lowered myself onto him again. I hadn't thought it possible for him to grow harder or larger, but he did both. And the flames inside of me threatened to turn into a wildfire.

With a moan, Roman dragged his mouth away from mine. "We need a new condom."

"Yes." I glanced around.

"In my pants pocket."

I lifted my hips, nearly groaning in disappointment when he was no longer inside of me. While I located the condom and removed it from the package, Roman, in spite of his "shackles," managed to dispose of the old one.

I sheathed him then, treating myself to the feel of the hard length of him as I did. There was a part of me that wanted to linger—to taste, to savor. But there was an aching emptiness inside of me, driving me. Placing my hands on his shoulders, I straddled him and slowly sank onto him. Each second of my descent was a delicious torture until he completely filled me. Our mouths met then, hot and wet and hungry. And my hips began to piston up and down.

I heard the rip of his shirt, and suddenly I was beneath him. We rolled across the floor, into thin streams of moonlight and out. I was as desperate as he, my hands as greedy. If it was a battle, we were both winning. Finally, trying to keep a grip on my sanity, I rose over him again. His fingers dug into my hips as we found that perfect speed and rhythm. My vision grayed, but his eyes were locked on mine as the madness took us.

7

I STOOD ALONE in the open doorway of my balcony. In the distance, the Ionian Sea gleamed bright blue in the morning sunshine, but my thoughts were still trapped in memories of the night Roman and I had spent together. Just thinking about what we'd done to each other was enough to heat my skin and melt parts of my body.

The word *insatiable* had taken on a new meaning for me. I'd learned things about myself and about my appetites that had shocked me. And driven me to learn more.

Together, we'd been like greedy children gorging ourselves on forbidden treats. The sky had been turning light and birds had been chirping when we'd finally fallen asleep. My last thought was that I fully understood Shakespeare's Juliet when she'd cursed the lark that heralded the dawn.

I'd taken some time in the bathroom to study myself in the mirror. The seeds of change I'd sensed in myself when I'd decided to proposition Roman for the second time at dinner had come to fruition during the night. I wasn't the same Philly I'd been before I'd come to Corfu. Something about being here on this island had made me...what? Stop dithering and decide to grab what the Fates were offering. My lips curved. That's exactly the way my aunt Cass would put it.

I realized now that I'd given up way too easily when I'd visited Roman's hospital room a month ago. I'd believed his lie and run away. Maybe I'd still been running by coming here to Greece. But I wasn't going to run anymore. I'd found exactly what I wanted.

I heard the sound of the tap stop and knew that Roman had finished shaving. I very nearly sighed. In a matter of minutes we'd leave the world we'd created during the night and have to deal with the day.

As if on cue, the young man from the beach suddenly stepped out of the woods and began to cut a diagonal path toward the villa. The white cat—Ariel—followed him. She was still very worried. And tired.

She seemed to sense my presence and glanced up at me. I calmed my mind, and once again the image of the white cat lying in the dark place filled it.

Caliban? I asked her.

Yes.

Then she disappeared from my sight beneath the balcony.

I sensed Roman's presence even before he touched my shoulder and ran his hand down my arm to link it with mine. I tried very hard not to let the casual intimacy of the gesture soften something deep inside of me.

"Your cousin returns," he murmured.

"Looks like."

Alexi—if it was him—looked tired and even younger than he'd appeared to be through my camera lens. He was wearing a T-shirt and what seemed to be the same shorts he'd worn on the beach the day before. He'd covered half the distance to the hotel when Miranda rushed across the lawn to meet him.

"You can't come in." Her tone was hushed, urgent.

Roman drew me back from the edge of the balcony so that we were out of sight, but we continued to eavesdrop.

"Why not?" Alexi asked.

"Inspector Ionescu is here looking for you. I told him you hadn't returned. His men are searching your room right now. And Mr. Delos's room. It was just luck that I saw you from the kitchen window. Go."

Alexi ran a hand through his hair. "Has Magellan filed another complaint that I've been hanging around his precious *castello* and poking around his caves? Delos was hanging out in those caves more than I was. And Magellan can't press charges against me for trespassing on his precious estate. I haven't been able to get past the gate. Only Ariel slips through. She's trying to lead me to Caliban. I know it. But the guards won't let me in."

"This doesn't have anything to do with Mr. Magellan. It's about the man you were arguing with on the beach yesterday."

"Delos?"

"Then it *was* you?" Miranda began to wring her hands. "I knew it."

"So I argued with Delos. That's not a crime."

"He was shot. Killed. That's why the police are searching his room."

Alexi seemed stunned into silence—but only for a moment. "Well, I didn't shoot him."

"You were there. Your cousin Philly Angelis saw you through the lens of her camera. She says you shoved him, knocked him down. And you didn't come home last night."

"I spent the night looking for Caliban."

"Inspector Ionescu must suspect you had something to do with Mr. Delos's death." Miranda sounded panicked.

"Mom, I didn't shoot Mr. Delos." Alexi's tone had gentled and he placed his hands on his mother's shoulders. "Sure, I argued with him. He told me he'd seen Caliban in one of those caves beneath the Castello, but he wouldn't show me which one. He said he had to get back here and make a call because his cell wouldn't work. I was angry. Furious. But I didn't shoot him. C'mon, we'll go inside and I'll talk to the inspector. It's going to be all right."

The moment I heard the door to the villa close, I turned to Roman. "Miranda knew who the dead man was all along."

"Yes." Roman's tone was thoughtful. "But she's worried about her son and perhaps a bit overprotective now that he's all she has left of her family. And Alexi evidently has a temper."

Whatever else Roman might have said was interrupted when Ariel suddenly appeared on our balcony railing. Again I calmed my mind and opened it. At first, I felt only her emotions. Frustration and anxiety were foremost.

Help.

Caliban is injured?

The image flashed into my mind of the barrel of a gun smashing down on a white cat's leg. "I think her brother's leg is broken. That's why he's lying so still and he can't get home," I murmured to Roman.

Ariel sat very still on the balcony watching us both.

"She told you that?" Roman asked softly.

"Not in words. I saw him getting hit by the barrel of a gun. Whoever did it must have left him in one of the caves. And you heard Alexi say that Delos had seen him there—and just left him." I felt a wave of empathy for my cousin and a wave of anger at the indifference of Delos. "No wonder Alexi shoved Delos to the ground. I might have done the same myself."

Ariel was sending more images now. In some of them the light was better. It seemed to be coming from above. Once again I saw the white cat lying very still in dappled sunlight. In most of them Ariel was sitting beside him. In one she had a small animal in her mouth. As far as I could make out they were on some kind of ledge.

"She's bringing him food, and there's water there," I said softly to Roman. "He doesn't seem to be in any immediate danger."

Help.

"But she's worried."

A knock sounded at the door. Releasing my hand, Roman went to open it. "Good morning, Demetria."

Over my shoulder, I saw Demetria beam a smile at him. "Mr. Angelis, Mrs. Kostas said to fetch you. Inspector Ionescu is here. He wants to talk with you."

"We'll be right there."

I turned back to Ariel. *I can't come right now.* I felt her frustration and disappointment so strongly that I nearly took a step back.

I tried to reassure her. *I'll come as soon as I can. I'll look for you on the beach where we were yesterday.* I pictured the crescent-shaped stretch of sand as clearly as I could in my mind. I hoped that she understood as she leaped to the branches of a nearby cypress tree and then disappeared.

AS IT TURNED OUT, Roman and I had to wait our turn to talk to Inspector Ionescu. When Demetria led us out onto the terrace, he was seated at the same table he'd used yesterday. It was located at the far end, isolated from the other tables. This time Alexi sat across from him. There were two men in uniform standing behind my cousin.

I didn't think that looked good and said as much to Roman once Demetria had served us coffee.

"I agree," Roman said. "Alexi is most likely the last person to have seen Delos alive. Add to that the fact that you saw him shove the victim to the ground moments before he was shot, and that elevates your cousin to the prime suspect."

My stomach twisted and I set down my coffee without tasting it. "He didn't have a gun."

"Not that you saw. But he was carrying a backpack."

I frowned at him. "You sound like you're building a case against him."

"I'm just trying to think the way a policeman would."

I glanced over at Alexi. The table was far enough away that it was impossible to overhear anything. The inspector seemed to be doing most of the talking.

"Ionescu's a smart man," Roman continued. "He has to know that Miranda recognized the description you gave of the younger man on the beach. He probably suspects that she recognized the description of Delos also. Policemen get annoyed when they're lied to. He's not going to be happy with us, either."

"What do you mean?"

"I imagine you were right on the money and he Googled Kit Angelis the moment he got back to his office. Your brother and I don't look anything alike."

"I told you to tell him the truth."

"You could have ratted me out."

But I hadn't. Instead I'd backed up his lie. "Do you think he'll arrest us?"

Roman reached across the table and gave my hand a squeeze. "I hope not. I called Kit yesterday when Ionescu was questioning you and gave him a heads-up about what was going on here. I also called my father. I imagine the inspector knows exactly who I am by now."

Just then the inspector joined us. "Mr. Oliver, Ms. Angelis."

The jig was obviously up. The moment Ionescu sat

down, Demetria placed his coffee in front of him. He sipped it, then met Roman's eyes. "Why did you lie about who you were yesterday?"

"Mrs. Kostas didn't have any rooms. She was going to put me up somewhere in the village. Since she's related to Philly, and I understand she's had a very traditional Greek upbringing, I thought she might have concerns about my sharing a room with her. But I wasn't about to let Philly stay here alone after someone took a shot at her."

Ionescu turned to me. "You went along with the lie Mr. Oliver told Mrs. Kostas."

"Yes."

"Why?"

I met his eyes squarely. "Because I wanted Roman to stay with me."

"I see." He sipped his coffee, then asked, "Is the young man seated in front of my men the same person you saw arguing with the man in the wide-brimmed hat on the beach?"

"Yes."

"But you didn't know it was your cousin Alexi?"

"I'd never met him before. We still haven't been formally introduced."

Inspector Ionescu studied me for a moment as if he was weighing the truth of my explanation. I could feel heat staining my cheeks—I'd given him good reason to doubt my honesty.

"You've found out the identity of the dead man?" Roman interrupted.

Ionescu shifted his gaze to Roman. "Antony Delos. He was a guest here at the Villa Prospero for the past five days. His body was recovered by a fisherman early this morning about three miles down the coast. But I had already tracked his identity through his cell."

"What have you found out about him?"

Ionescu paused to take another sip of coffee. "I know you are an astute businessman, Mr. Oliver. I also know you have powerful contacts here in Greece. This morning, I received several phone calls—one from a Detective Nik Angelis with the San Francisco Police Department, and another from Gianni Stassis. Both gave you glowing character references."

"You know of Stassis?" Roman asked.

Ionescu shrugged. "We're not quite so isolated here as you might think. He's one of the richest men in Greece and he's politically well connected. I dare say there are very few people in my country who would not recognize the name. I'd like to make a deal with you."

"What kind of deal?"

"Normally, I don't share information about an ongoing investigation. But in this instance, I'll fill you in on what I know so far about Antony Delos on the understanding that you'll share any information you can gather through Stassis and your other contacts."

For a moment, Roman said nothing. Mentally, I urged him to make the deal. If indeed my cousin Alexi was a prime suspect, then we needed as much information as possible to help him.

"You believe that through Stassis I can gather information that you can't?"

"What I believe is that you can access it more quickly." He glanced at Alexi, then turned his attention back to Roman. "And because you have a family connection, I'm sure you can see the advantage of that."

"You can't believe that Alexi had something to do with Antony Delos's murder," I said.

Ionescu's eyes, when they met mine, had the same flat

expression that my brother Nik's eyes always had when he was in cop mode. "What I believe doesn't matter, Ms. Angelis. I have to go with the evidence."

I swallowed hard when I realized that I'd supplied much of the evidence.

"Deal," Roman said. "What have you found out about Antony Delos?"

"He used to work for Interpol, mostly on high-profile gem thefts. Five years ago, he went private. He was still doing the same work, but for insurance companies and even more frequently for the well-heeled victims of the thefts. I did a little checking. The last call placed on his cell was to Carlo Ferrante, an Italian billionaire whose villa in Tuscany was robbed of a fortune in jewels six days ago. Five days ago, Delos checked into the Villa Prospero. I don't believe in coincidences, do you, Mr. Oliver?"

Something tightened in my stomach. Inspector Ionescu couldn't suspect that Alexi or Miranda had something to do with the theft? I glanced over at my cousin again. He looked young and scared, hardly the picture of an international jewel thief.

Roman seemed equally unconvinced. "I remember reading about that jewel heist. The *Wall Street Journal* did an article on it complete with photos."

Ionescu nodded. "I don't know how detailed the article was, but the jewels have been in the Ferrante family for centuries, and they have an interesting history. Reputedly, they were part of a dowry when a Ferrante son married a French aristocrat in the fifteenth century. They've been passed down to the male heirs ever since. And this is the second time they've been stolen from Carlo Ferrante."

"I don't recall reading that," Roman said.

"The first time, they were snatched from a museum in Belgium. Ferrante had loaned them out as part of an exhibition of medieval jewelry. Six months later, they were miraculously and anonymously returned to him by the thief. Ferrante returned the small fortune he'd collected from the insurance company."

"Any idea of how Delos tracked the jewels to Corfu?"

For the first time since he'd seated himself at our table, the inspector smiled. "I'm hoping you can find out, Mr. Oliver. I couldn't get Mr. Ferrante to take my call. But he might take a call from Gianni Stassis. Perhaps, you might be able to expedite matters on that front?"

"What's in it for me?"

I stared at Roman. My contacts with him had all been social—either at my family's restaurant or at our fishing cabin. For the first time, I was catching a glimpse of the cool, ruthless businessman I'd heard Kit brag so often about.

The blunt question didn't bother the inspector at all. In fact, his smile grew wider. "For starters, I won't mention to Mrs. Kostas that you're not Ms. Angelis's brother. I agree with you that she shouldn't be alone until this matter is cleared up." Then his expression sobered. "And the sooner we find out who shot Antony Delos, the safer Ms. Angelis will be."

I was getting a little tired of being left out of the conversation, but before I could say anything, two men in uniform strode onto the terrace and came directly to our table.

"Someone searched Mr. Delos's room before we got there," the taller one said.

The other one wore gloves and lifted the rifle he was carrying. "We found this in Mr. Kostas's room."

Ionescu rose and moved to the table where Alexi was still seated in front of the other two policemen.

"Alexi, you'll have to come down to the station with me."

Miranda rushed over to her son, and I sprang from my chair to join her.

"You can't think that he shot Mr. Delos," I said to the inspector. "The man with the rifle was high up on the cliff face, close to the Castello. I can testify to that."

The inspector ignored my outburst and I stood staring, horrified as the two uniformed men assisted my cousin to his feet and escorted him off the terrace. All of the breakfast conversation had stopped. Everyone was watching as Inspector Ionescu followed Alexi out of sight. Miranda started to weep softly, and I didn't know what to say, what to do. It was Roman who went to her and simply folded her into his arms.

I felt my heart take a little tumble and that alarm sounded in the back of my mind again.

IT WAS NEARLY an hour later that Roman finished making calls. I inferred from eavesdropping on his side of the conversation that he'd asked Stassis to recommend a local attorney to represent Alexi. When I'd passed on that information to Miranda, it had done a great deal to settle her. Roman had even thought to call Kit and ask him to do research on Carlo Ferrante and both thefts of his family's jewels. The man thought of everything.

In the meantime, the only thing I'd done was to hold my cousin Miranda's hand and try to reassure her that Alexi would be home soon. Something that I was not at all sure of myself. Ever since he'd been escorted out of the Villa Prospero, questions had been spinning through my mind. What had he been doing with that gun? Why hadn't he returned home until this morning?

I turned to Miranda and asked the question that only she

could answer. "Why did you lie to Inspector Ionescu yesterday? You knew from my descriptions that I'd seen Alexi and Mr. Delos arguing on the beach."

She slipped her hand from mine and clasped hers together. "I was so worried about Alexi. He hasn't been himself since Caliban went missing. He loves those cats so much. They were a gift from his father shortly before he died." She turned to me and met my eyes. "Alexi's all I have left." Then she lifted her chin. "But he wouldn't shoot anyone. He doesn't even have a gun."

What she said made sense to me. The young man I'd seen on the beach had acted impulsively out of anger. And from what I'd learned since then, with good reason. But whoever had shot Antony Delos had chosen a spot on the cliff side and taken careful aim.

Unless… Questions erupted in my mind again. What if Alexi's absences from the Villa Prospero hadn't had anything to do with the missing Caliban? What if he'd been involved in something else altogether? Guilt flooded through me. I hadn't even formally met Alexi and I was suspecting him of somehow being involved in a major jewelry theft.

Seeing that Roman had finally repocketed his cell, I asked, "How long will it be before you hear back from Stassis?"

Roman shrugged. "Hard to tell. I asked for a private meeting with Carlo Ferrante."

My eyes widened.

"Might as well ask for the moon. Ionescu wants to know why Delos came here the day after the robbery. I'd like to know that, too." He shifted his gaze to Miranda. "What can you tell me about Antony Delos? What kind of a guest was he?"

A line appeared on Miranda's forehead as she considered. "I thought of him as an ideal one. Quiet, kept to himself. He ate breakfast early, always requested a packed lunch, and he'd be gone for the whole day, exploring the island. When Caliban disappeared, Alexi asked him to keep an eye out for him. Mr. Delos agreed. I don't understand why anyone would want to shoot him."

"Did he ever mention why he came here? Why he chose the Villa Prospero?"

Miranda shook her head.

Roman looked at me. I noted that he hadn't mentioned anything about the jewel theft to Miranda. But why do that if it wasn't necessary? It would only make her worry more. Roman might be ruthless in his business dealings, but there was an innate kindness about him that had my admiration for him rising even higher.

"Ferrante might very well have some information about what brought Delos to the Villa Prospero," Roman said. "But Stassis is going to have to call in some favors. Apparently, Ferrante's eccentric and a bit of a recluse. It may take a while, and in the meantime, we wait."

"Alexi is going to be so worried about the cats," Miranda said. "He's so sure that Caliban is still alive, that he's trapped somehow in one of the caves beneath the Castello."

"He is alive," I said. "But his leg is injured. He can't move, but Ariel has been bringing him food, and there's water."

Miranda blinked and stared at me. "How do you know?"

"Philly has a psychic gift with animals," Roman explained. "She can communicate with them."

"You talk to them?"

"Something like that," I said. Miranda's tone was skeptical, but I was used to that kind of reaction.

Then she frowned and pressed her fingers against her temples. "Oh, yes. Yes, of course. Your father and Helena told me how special powers ran in your mother's family. He told me about your ability. But I'd forgotten all of this…"

When she dropped her hands to the table, I covered one of them with mine. Then I filled Miranda in on everything else that I'd learned from Ariel.

Miranda nodded when I'd finished. "Alexi says that she disappears through the gates of the Castello or over the wall. Some of the caves are reputed to have two entrances—one on the cliff side and another farther up the hill. He's so frustrated that Mr. Magellan won't let him onto the estate to look for the second entrance. And Mr. Magellan is furious with him."

I recalled the scene I'd eavesdropped on when I'd first arrived at the Villa Prospero.

"He's filed several complaints against Alexi," Miranda continued. "He has all the caves posted with No Trespassing signs. They're dangerous because when the tide comes in many of them fill with water and escape becomes impossible."

"What was Mr. Delos's relationship with the cats? Did they get along?" Roman asked.

A small line appeared on Miranda's forehead as she considered. "Now that you mention it, he always took the time to talk to them."

"Did they ever go off with him on his explorations?"

"They may have. I didn't pay much attention."

I turned to Roman. "I need to find Ariel. I promised that I would try to meet her on the beach where we were yesterday."

This was something that I purposefully hadn't mentioned to him earlier to give him less time to argue. I kept my eyes on Roman's, trying to make my case. "It was about this time yesterday when she was down there with

Mr. Delos, and they'd evidently been in the caves. If Miranda is right and there's more than one entrance to the cave Caliban is trapped in, we should check it out."

"I don't like the idea of visiting the beach where someone tried to shoot you yesterday."

"Why would the shooter expect me to come back? And if we don't find Ariel, we'll leave."

"Until we know more about what's going on, it's too dangerous."

I rose, meeting his eyes steadily. "I'm going to the beach. I promised Ariel I would come."

Finally, Roman nodded, and I felt as if I'd just won a major negotiation.

Miranda rose as we did. "I'll pack you something to eat just in case you miss lunch."

I was about to tell her not to bother, but she was already hurrying away.

"She's an innkeeper," Roman murmured. "She'll feel better if she makes us something. And she needs things to do to keep her mind off of Alexi being at the police station."

I studied him for a moment. "Were you born with an innate knowledge of people or did you acquire it at Oliver Enterprises?"

His lips curved and he reached out to trail just the tips of his fingers down my arm. The touch was so gentle, nothing like the way he'd touched me during the night, but I felt the warmth right down to my toes. "A little of both, I suspect. You can't stay in business very long if you don't know people. Just as you couldn't build your clientele if you didn't know animals."

8

ON THEIR FAST DESCENT to the beach, Roman decided that Philly wasn't exactly the girl he thought he'd known for years. There were unexpected layers to her that he hadn't noticed before. The temper for one thing. He found that he enjoyed watching her struggle to rein it in. And she had a steely determination that he'd evidently blinded himself to before. He'd seen it in her eyes when she'd told him she had to go to the beach—he'd known that she would have gone without him.

But he'd also experienced that single-minded determination up close and personal when she'd seduced him last night. He wasn't sure how he'd allowed it to happen. He should have been able to keep his hands off of her—he'd had seven years of practice. Seven years to learn to live with the dull ache of always wanting her. Seven years of telling himself she was too young for him.

But she wasn't. She was a woman—a fascinating woman who knew what she wanted and went after it.

Last night he'd wanted to blame it on the damn dress, but it had been Philly who'd bewitched him. Philly who'd set fires inside of him that had burned out of control until they'd both been consumed by them. The thing was—what they'd done to each other in their room last night should have gotten her out of his system once and for all.

Instead, making love with Philly had seemed to imbed her so deeply in his psyche that he wondered if he'd ever be free of her. Hell, he wanted her again right now. There was a part of him—a part he hadn't known existed—that wanted to snatch her up, carry her off into the trees and make love to her. Caveman tactics had never been his style before.

When she reached the outcrop of rock that bordered the crescent-shaped stretch of sand, she turned back to him. "You're dragging your heels."

He joined her and took her hand in his. "You're right. I'm having second thoughts about this whole thing. I wish I could talk you into going back to the villa."

"I need to talk to Ariel. As much as I believe that Caliban isn't in any immediate danger, we have to find out where he is and get him out of that cave."

Though the sun still beat down on all sides, the sea was turning angry and the rocks were becoming slick. Keeping her hand in his, he drew her over them and onto the sandy beach. Then he glanced out to sea. In the distance, black clouds were forming. "There's a storm blowing in."

She followed the direction of his gaze. "In Shakespeare's play, it was a storm and a shipwreck that brought Prospero to his island. Perhaps this one will bring us some luck." She pulled him with her across the sand. "I've been thinking."

"Yes?"

"Don't you think it's odd that Ionescu never once mentioned Andre Magellan's name with regard to the missing jewels and Delos's presence on the island?"

"Not particularly. I'm surprised that he told us as much as he did. He's a very canny man and in spite of the so-called deal he made with us, he's not going to reveal all his suspicions to a couple of relative strangers. Plus, I imagine that from a political standpoint, he has to tread lightly where Magellan is concerned. Those extravagant parties that the man throws have to bring a lot of tourist money to the area."

"But the caves Delos was evidently exploring lie below the Castello Corli, which belongs to Magellan. He's posted all of them, and he's been filing complaints because Alexi is hanging around them. I think that if I had a cache of stolen jewels to hide and hundreds of guests and servants poking around my house, those caves would make a perfect temporary hiding place. And I wouldn't want anyone hanging around them. You should have your friend Gianni Stassis check out Andre Magellan."

"I already asked him to," Roman said. "Kit's also re-searching Magellan's background."

"So I'm several steps behind you. Are you always on top of everything?"

"I do my best." And the person he wanted to be on top of right now was pulling him over another outcrop of rocks. On this side below the cliff face, the terrain was much rougher.

Philly scanned the stretch of rocks and boulders in front of them. "I was so sure she'd be on the beach. I pictured it as clearly as I could in my mind."

"Are you always sure the animals you communicate with get the message?"

"Not one hundred percent. Her disappointment that I couldn't come right away might have interfered. And her level of anxiety about her brother is very high."

Roman studied the sea. The clouds were getting closer, and while the waves were still quite a distance from the rocky cliff face, he had no idea how quickly the tide came in.

"Delos and Ariel must have been coming from one of the caves when Alexi stopped them," Philly said. "Let's check a few of them."

Without waiting for his agreement, she ducked her head and moved into the first one.

When she went a few steps farther into the cave, Roman crouched low and moved quickly to take her hand. "We don't have a flashlight, Philly."

"Let me just try to contact Ariel mentally." After a few moments, she sighed. "I can't sense her in this one."

Together they walked back out into the sunshine. There was a faint rumble of thunder, and he noted that the black clouds were moving fast.

"Let's just try a few more," Philly said.

Roman lost count of exactly how many they tried. Some of them weren't caves at all, but merely deep crevices that the sea had carved in the rock. They'd gone some distance when the heavens opened and the rain crashed down. By the time they reached the next cave and dashed in, they were drenched. Rain lashed into the opening of their shelter, and the walls seemed to amplify the sound of it beating against the rocks. Thunder rolled, and Roman urged her around a sharp corner and farther into the darkness.

"I have a feeling about this one," Philly said in a low tone. "I'm going to try to connect with her."

Roman settled his hands on her shoulders and waited. Minutes ticked by. A few feet behind them, the storm raged furiously.

Finally, Philly said, "I can sense something, someone. But it's not Ariel. Maybe it's Caliban, but the connection is so faint."

"Perhaps he's sleeping," Roman said.

She concentrated for a moment. "I can't tell. If we'd only thought to bring a flashlight."

Though understanding the frustration in her voice, Roman turned her to face him and said, "Once the rain lets up, we'll have to go back. I have no idea how fast the tide comes in, but I want us to be on the sand before we find out."

"I'm sorry this whole outing has been a bust. I was just so anxious to talk to Ariel, and I was certain she'd be here."

It was dark, but he could see the gleam of her eyes. He lifted a hand and brushed his knuckles along her jaw, then cupped his hand behind her head.

A tremor moved through her. "You're always touching me now. Even when you're not about to make love to me."

He framed her face with his hands. "I can't seem to help myself. Whenever I'm near you, I want my hands on you. Do you mind?"

"No—no."

"More than that, every time I'm near you, I want to be inside of you."

"Roman."

His name trembled out of her on a breath, and the fire that he'd managed to keep banked the whole time they'd searched the caves burst free.

"I want you inside of me."

Clamping down on his control, he nibbled his way to her ear and whispered, "I will be soon. I've been wanting you ever since the last time I had you. And I'm going to take you here. Right now."

HIS WORDS, his tone had my knees melting and my head reeling. I wouldn't have been able to stand if my back hadn't been pressed against the wall of the cave. I couldn't even lift my hands to help him with my clothes.

"I thought of doing this at least a dozen times on the path to the beach." He used his teeth and tongue on my throat while his hands efficiently stripped me out of my shirt, bra and shorts. "I don't know what it is about you, but I can't seem to get enough."

The words sent ripples of pleasure through me. "Not a problem."

When he ran his palms over my throat, my breasts and down my sides, I moaned his name.

The rain had eased enough for me to hear the ragged sound of our breathing, and when I heard his zipper go down, everything inside of me tightened in anticipation.

"Now."

I somehow found the strength to wrap my arms around him. The next thing I knew he was kneeling on the floor of the cave, and I was straddling his thighs. Time seemed to stretch endlessly as he sheathed himself with a condom. Then at last, he lifted my hips and pushed into me. I snaked my legs around him and took even more of him in as my mouth sought his.

"Are you all right?" His voice was rough with an underlying urgency.

"Fine. But you can't be." I recalled how uneven the floor of the cave had been when we'd entered. "The rocks."

He whispered against my lips, "Make me forget them."

I did my best, using my mouth on his body. He dug his fingers into my hips, lifting me and withdrawing so that he could push back into me very slowly.

"Faster."

"Not yet."

He kept the rhythm agonizingly slow, torturing us both. Each time I teetered on the brink of release, he would pause.

"Now." I fought against the pressure of his hands as he lifted my hips.

His laugh was wicked, infuriating, and only stoked the fires burning inside of me. Desperate, I sank my teeth into his earlobe at the same instant that I slid my hands beneath his shorts and dug my fingernails into his buttocks.

He moved faster then, and I matched him thrust for thrust until the climax slammed into us both and our simultaneous cries echoed and reechoed off the walls of the cave.

WHEN MY BRAIN CELLS finally began to click on again, I was sitting on Roman's lap on the floor of the cave. The light was brighter now. The storm had blown over and sunlight poured through the mouth of the cave. I was naked except for my shoes, but he was still fully clothed.

When I stirred, he tipped my face so that our eyes met.

"I can't keep my hands off of you."

I saw concern in his eyes, so I lifted my hand to rest it on his cheek and smiled. "That's okay. I want your hands on me."

"I've never experienced this lack of control with a woman before. I don't want to hurt you."

"I don't think you could. Besides, we have a deal. There isn't anything we can't do to each other for as long as we're here in Greece."

"That's not what I meant, Philly. I'm talking about when we leave."

Alarm bells went off in my mind and panic knotted in my stomach as I pressed my fingers against his lips. I knew what he was going to say—that what we were sharing had to be temporary. But in spite of all my resolve, I found it too hard to hear the words. "We're not going to talk about what comes later. I don't want to spoil one second of the time that we have here together. I'm a big girl, Roman. I'll keep my word."

For a moment, he looked as if he was going to say more, but when he did speak it was to say, "We'd better get you back in your clothes and move out in the sunshine so that we can both dry off."

The moment we exited the cave, I tried to put Roman's words and every thought of the future out of my mind by focusing my attention on the glorious day. The sky was so clear that I thought for a moment I might have imagined the storm. The sea had moved closer, the waves stretching their length to a few yards from where we now stood.

"The backpack," Roman murmured and walked into the cave.

I turned to watch him, and something—a flash of sunlight off metal—caught my eye. Later, I would think that it was pure luck that had me notice it. Or the Fates.

I moved closer to the entrance of the cave. "Roman?"

When he joined me, I pointed to what I was looking at and we both moved closer. It was a small cylinder of metal no longer than an inch and it was taped to one corner of the cave opening.

"What is that?" I asked.

"My guess would be that it's some kind of state-of-the-art surveillance camera."

I reached for his hand and gripped it hard. "It didn't get pictures of us making love, did it?"

"No. We'd moved too far inside to get out of the storm. But I'm betting that it caught us entering and exiting."

"Someone's interested in whoever goes in and out? Why?"

"Good question." Roman turned then, scanning the area. "We're getting out of here. Whoever is on the receiving end of that surveillance camera spotted us going into that cave over twenty minutes ago." Tightening his grip on my hand, he pulled me closer to the cliff face.

"I wonder if all of the caves have cameras."

"I was thinking the same thing."

We checked three, but found nothing. By that time we'd

only covered half the distance back, and some of the waves were reaching our shoes.

"Roman, if we go on the assumption that Antony Delos explored that particular cave, whoever was on the other end of that surveillance equipment knew it. And there was a sniper on that hill waiting for him when he appeared on the beach."

"Yeah. I'm thinking there's been plenty of time for a sniper to take up his position for us."

I shivered. "I was hoping you'd say that you think I'm being paranoid."

"What I think is that I never should have agreed to bring you here. So here's the plan. Once we get to the rocks, we're going to stash the backpack someplace high. Then we're going all the way out to the end of the rocks and we'll swim across the cove. That should put us out of the range of any rifle shots. You game?"

"Yes." It was a good plan. And I was a much better swimmer than I'd been at sixteen. My brothers and father had seen to that.

We were still a good two hundred yards from our goal when Ariel appeared on the outcrop of rock. She raced toward us. When she stopped a few feet away, I crouched down. *I've been looking for you.*

This way. She tried to walk around us, but a wave crashed over my shoes and sent her scooting up on a rock. I looked behind us and saw that the waves were now sweeping up against the cliff face. The tide was coming in with a vengeance.

"We can't go back now," Roman said. "Remember what Miranda said about the caves filling up with water?"

I did. Vividly. I thought of Caliban. But if he was in one of the caves, he had to be high enough up to be safe from the tides if he'd survived for two days already. Maybe that was why the connection I'd felt had been so faint—because he'd been so far away. Leaning over, I focused my attention on Ariel.

We can't go there right now. We'll have to come back once the tide goes out.

An image filled my mind. There was enough light this time that I could see the edge of a rock ledge. Caliban was stretched out on his side, and one of his legs was at an odd angle. His eyes were closed, but I could see the steady rise and fall of his rib cage.

Roman suddenly grabbed my arm and drew me up. "We've got company."

Following his gaze, I saw the boat. It was coming from the end of the rock outcrop, and it was headed in our direction. I felt something fly by my face and heard a ping behind me even as I registered that the man standing in the prow of the boat had a rifle.

There was another ping, I ducked—and Ariel leaped off the boulder she was perched on. *This way.* She began jumping from one rock to the next in the direction she'd come from.

"She's taking us somewhere." I yanked Roman along as I began to run after her.

"I hope it isn't far." He shifted so that his body blocked mine from the shooter as we raced after the cat. We scrambled frantically over the wet rocks, slipped as we tried to keep our bodies close to the ground.

The man in the boat kept sending bullets our way. I figured the only reason he didn't hit all three of us was that the movement of the boat must be having an effect on his aim. We'd nearly reached the ridge of rocks when Roman said, "We're never going to make it over them. They'll slow us down, and he'll be able to pick us off like clay pigeons."

"The cave," I said as we neared the first one I'd ducked into.

This way. Ariel dashed into it.

Roman and I both had to crouch low as we followed her into the darkness. Behind us, I heard the whine of another bullet as it hit the cave entrance.

9

ARIEL HAD COMPLETELY disappeared into the darkness of the cave.

This way.

Before I could relay her request to Roman, he edged his way back to the entrance. This cave was much smaller than the one with the surveillance camera. I was about five-two, and I couldn't stand up straight. If I stretched out my hands I could touch both walls. The rocks were damp.

"There's one good thing," Roman called over his shoulder. "They can't land their boat here. The rocks would tear it to pieces. On the other hand, they don't have to land the boat. They don't even have to bother about shooting us. As long as they can keep us trapped here, the tide will finish the job for them."

He moved back to me and took my hands. "We have two choices—stay here and take our chances with the tide or make a run for it. I'm favoring the latter. Their aim has been off so far, and our luck may hold."

"Ariel wants us to follow her," I told Roman. "Miranda said that some of these caves have more than one entrance. Maybe Ariel knows another way out."

As if on cue, Ariel appeared out of the darkness and threaded her way around my ankles.

A wave crashed through the cave entrance, sending spray against the granite walls.

"She's going to lead us out," I said to Roman.

"You're sure about this?"

"I trust her."

He hesitated for one moment, then nodded. "I trust you."

And that was how our journey began, with Ariel in the lead and Roman bringing up the rear. We made a very slow-moving parade. Surrounded by total darkness, we were forced to feel our way carefully along. I had one hand in front of me, the other running along the side of the cave. The slabs of rock that formed the walls were worn smooth in places but remained rough in others. As we inched our way along, I became aware of two things—we were climbing upward and the cave itself was gradually narrowing on all sides. I was crouched so low now that I was practically crab walking. The fact that the space was shrinking to tunnel-like proportions worried me. What if there was a way out for Ariel but not for Roman and me?

I figured we'd gone about a hundred yards or so when I was forced to drop to my knees. "I have to crawl," I informed Roman.

"I've been doing that for a while now." He didn't say anything else, but I knew he also had to be wondering what we were going to do if the passage became too small for us.

We didn't have the breath to talk much after that. The incline became much steeper and rocks were cutting into my hands and my knees. Sweat was pouring off me. Then without any warning, my head rapped sharply into a rock that seemed to lie in the direct center of the little tunnel we were crawling through. Panic streamed through me. Had we come to some kind of dead end? There'd be no retreat. The tide had probably already filled the lower part of the cave.

Then I felt Roman's hand on the small of my back. He rubbed it gently. "What is it?"

Just the tone of his voice and his touch helped me to push down the rush of fear I was feeling and I ran my hand slowly over the slab of rock I'd smacked into. Not a solid wall. There was open space on either side of it.

"The cave branches off here. We can go left or right." And I hadn't a clue which way Ariel had taken.

"Ask Ariel," Roman suggested.

Of course. I would have thought of that—the moment my little panic attack was over. I forced myself to focus and willed the remnants of my fear away. *Ariel? Which way?*

I was kneeling with one hand in each tunnel when I felt her brush against my right hand. Relief streamed through me.

Then she was gone.

"To the right," I told Roman.

The bad news was that the new tunnel was even smaller than the one we'd left. Every few feet, my shoulders brushed against rock. If the space was becoming a tight fit for me, it had to be even more uncomfortable for Roman.

"I'm ditching the backpack," Roman said.

After that, neither of us spoke for a while. We needed all of our energy because we were crawling at such a steep incline.

My shoulders ached, and I had begun to pant. My hands had become so slick with sweat that they slipped out from under me and I landed flat on my stomach. What breath was left in my lungs whooshed out, and I was afraid that I wouldn't get it back.

"Don't give up now," Roman said from behind me. "The exit can't be much farther."

"Right," I wheezed and with muscles trembling I managed to haul myself back up on my knees. For a while,

I emptied my mind and focused on putting one hand in front of the other. If Roman hadn't been behind me, I might not have kept going. Every once in a while, his hand would brush my ankle or my calf.

Then I whacked my head against a second rock. This time I didn't waste time panicking. I ran my hands over it quickly. "There's a slab of rock jutting out into the tunnel. We're going to have to wiggle our way around it." So saying, I stretched out full length, rolled to my side and began to muscle my way past the rock an inch at a time.

Once I was on the other side I crawled a few yards and waited for Roman. "It's a tight squeeze."

"Tell me about it." He sounded as breathless as I did.

He swore once, grunted several times and swore again before I once more felt him behind me.

It wasn't until then that I realized I could see my hands on the floor of the cave. And when I glanced up, I actually saw sunlight. Still, it seemed to take forever to reach the opening. My stomach tightened when I saw how narrow it was. I eased myself onto my stomach again and wriggled my upper body out. Then I grabbed shrubs and anything else I could get my hands on to drag myself all the way out onto grass.

Breathing deeply, I turned around and grabbed Roman's outstretched hands, braced my feet against a nearby tree trunk and pulled. His head appeared next. He had to roll sideways and hunch his shoulders to make any further progress. It was slow going. We had to fight for every inch.

Sweat was pouring off of him, and his shirt was torn in two places before we finally got him out. He immediately rolled over onto his back and pulled me on top of him. For a long time we just clung to each other. Even when my heart had stopped racing, I didn't want to move. Roman's arms were around me and every inch of my body was molded to his. Yet, I experienced none of the fire and passion that I'd felt every other time he'd held me. Instead, a river of warmth moved through me, and I felt as if I was coming home. My heart didn't tumble this time. It plummeted.

He's the one.

No. Ignore it, Philly. It's because you both just escaped death. That's all. But I knew I was lying to myself. In spite of all my resolve and everything I'd promised, I was falling in love with Roman. And I was going to have to figure out what to do about that.

To escape my thoughts, I said, "I never want to do something like that again."

Roman's arms tightened around me. "We're on the same page there."

We'd nearly died. Neither of us said it, but the thought hung in the air between us.

I finally found the energy to raise my head and look down at him. His face was dirty, and his hair stood out every which way. He didn't look at all like the Roman I'd known for years. "You look terrible." And I was fascinated. I had it really bad for Roman Oliver.

One of his eyebrows quirked upward. "Do you want me to tell you how you look?"

"A gentleman wouldn't do that to a lady."

"A lady would be able to take the truth."

"Lucky for me I'm not a lady." Then I laughed and hugged him hard. When he joined in the laughter, I felt the last of my fears melt away.

The sun was pouring down, the air carried the scent of lemons, and the horror of what had almost happened in the cave was fading. "I am so glad we made it. We owe Ariel our lives." I glanced around, but she hadn't spoken to me since we'd both wiggled out of that opening.

Roman's expression sobered then. He sat up, drawing me with him. "Philly, this is the second time someone's tried to kill you. I want to take you away from here."

I framed his dirty face with my hands. "I know. And there's a part of me that wants to run away, too. But Ariel just saved our lives, and the least I can do is rescue Caliban for her. Plus, we can't leave Miranda while Alexi is suspected of murder."

"I knew that's what you'd say. But I want your word you won't go back to the beach or the caves again. It's too dangerous."

"You have my word." I wasn't stupid. It would be much too risky to try to revisit the cave with the surveillance camera even after the tide had gone out. I'd have to find another way of rescuing Caliban, who I was now certain was lying injured on a rock ledge in that cave.

"C'mon." Roman took my hand as we both made it a little unsteadily to our feet. "I won't completely feel safe until I get you back to the Villa Prospero."

Roman moved slowly through the trees, and we hadn't gone more than fifty yards or so when I saw a wall of stone to our left.

"That's the Castello Corli," I said.

The cypress trees had begun to thin, and Roman and I caught a glimpse of a road ahead. When we reached it, we saw the entrance to the Castello to our left. The gate was made of iron and looked as ancient and impenetrable as the stone wall of the old fortress that bordered it on each side. I counted three men on guard duty, one in a shack and two standing as sentinels at each end of the gate. All three carried rifles.

"That's heavy-duty security," I murmured to Roman. Then I spotted Ariel perched on the top of the wall no more than twenty feet above one of the guards' heads. I started toward her, but I'd barely taken two steps before Roman grabbed my arm and drew me back into the trees.

"We can't go to her. Until we find out who just shot at us and trapped us in that cave, the safest route we can take is to let them think we drowned."

"Good plan. Good thing I'm in this mess with a strategy-minded CEO."

Roman sent me a sideways glance. "We have our uses."

A car appeared to our right, coming fast and sending dust and gravel spewing into the trees and shrubs that lined the road. I immediately recognized the sporty red convertible I'd seen on my arrival at the Villa Prospero, and Andre Magellan was seated behind the wheel. The shirt he wore today was as flashy as the one he'd worn the day before—a wild print in shades of royal blue, red and yellow.

The brakes squealed as he stopped at the iron gates. The guards scrambled to open them, and Magellan shot out of the car and yelled at them. He spoke in Greek, and gestured toward Ariel.

I quickly established a mental link with her because I wasn't sure whether or not she could see Roman and me.

Ariel.

Her response came immediately. *This way.*

We can't. You go. Danger.

Even as I relayed the information, one of the guards ran to the side of Magellan's car and raised his rifle. Ariel leaped from the wall just as the shot exploded. The man in the shack took a second shot, then Magellan grabbed the rifle and fired two more rounds.

I was so furious that if Roman hadn't been still holding my arm, I would have raced forward.

"Easy," he said in a low tone. "She's a smart cat. Can you find out if she's all right?"

Pushing down my anger, I tried to link with her again. *Ariel?*

Her reply when it came was faint. *This way.*

The image flashed into my mind. It was the same rock ledge I'd seen before. In the weak sunlight, I could see that Caliban's eyes were open. For a moment, I felt the same faint connection that I'd experienced in the cave. I didn't experience the same level of distress that I felt from Ariel.

I'm sorry. We'll come back as soon as we can. Tell him that. Tell him not to give up. And be careful. There are bad men who want to hurt you.

I waited for a few more seconds, but there was nothing further. I turned to Roman. "She not only led us out of the cave, she's still trying to bring us to Caliban. There must be a second entrance to the cave he's in on the grounds of the Castello. I think she's spending as much time with him as she can. She should be safe as long as she stays there. But I wish there was some way we could just go and get both of them right now."

Roman squeezed my hand. "We can't. We need to report all of this to Inspector Ionescu, and I need to check in with Stassis."

AN HOUR LATER, just before two o'clock, Roman was seated next to Philly in Inspector Ionescu's office in the nearby town of Myrtos. The room was as neat as the man himself. There were two file cabinets and a desk with two metal chairs in front of it. Another chair stood against the wall near a small window that offered a view of a bustling, sun-splashed street. Today the inspector wore a pale tan suit with a white shirt and brown tie. His desk was clear save for his notebook.

Philly had just given him a summary of their cave adventure—their experience with the men in the boat who'd shot at them, and their harrowing escape from the tunnel Ariel had led them through.

Ionescu was still making meticulous notes.

To Roman's relief, they'd reached the Villa Prospero without further incident and found that Gianni Stassis had arranged a meeting in Athens with Carlo Ferrante. Stassis had even sent a car to take them to his private plane, which was waiting at a small airport ten miles outside of Myrtos. They were expected to join him later that afternoon on his yacht, which was anchored near Athens on the Ithaca coast.

The man worked fast, and Roman was grateful for it. He wanted Philly away from Corfu, and Stassis had provided the perfect excuse. Not that Philly had been eager to make the trip to Athens. They'd had their first argument. She'd wanted to stay until they'd figured out a way to rescue Caliban, but trying to gain access to the grounds of the Castello was problematic—not merely because they'd probably be refused. For the present, he still believed that it was best to let whoever had tried to kill them think they'd succeeded.

Knowing that she was concerned about the cats, he'd reminded her that, by her own account, neither cat was in any immediate danger and Ariel was watching over Caliban. He'd finally prevailed by telling her that when a business deal reached an impasse, the best strategy was to find another approach. Carlo Ferrante might very well provide a way to Andre Magellan.

Roman still wasn't certain what he would have done if Philly hadn't been convinced by his argument, but he was pretty sure caveman tactics would have been involved. The woman was bringing out qualities in him that he hadn't known he possessed.

As Ionescu continued to write, Roman studied Philly. She sat facing the inspector, her hands clasped tight in her lap. Luckily, most of the surface damage they'd suffered in their escape from the cave had washed away in the shower. Then they'd doctored up the scrapes and cuts on their hands and knees with the first-aid kit that Miranda had provided. By the time Stassis's driver had dropped them at the police station, Roman had felt almost human again.

For a moment, he let his mind return to their harrowing escape from the cave. Philly's courage hadn't wavered for a moment, nor had her belief in Ariel. He'd never met another woman like her.

Ionescu stopped writing and glanced up at Philly. "How many times did the man in the boat shoot at you?"

Philly glanced at Roman. "At least a dozen times, wouldn't you say?"

Roman nodded.

"Yet he didn't hit you."

"No," Philly said.

"So his purpose may have been to warn you away from the caves."

Philly stiffened in her chair. "Or to force us into one of the caves so the tide could drown us."

"The more I think of it," Roman said, "the more I believe that might have been their intention. To have two more people killed by snipers in a twenty-four-hour period might have focused too much police attention on the Castello. But a couple of tourists who ignored the posted signs and drowned in one of the caves—that would have been a terrible tragedy. And it would seem to have no connection with Antony Delos's death."

Ionescu made a sound that might have signaled agreement.

Philly leaned forward in her chair. "Whatever is going

on, that cave with the surveillance camera is at the center of it. I also believe that my cousin's cat Caliban is lying on a rock ledge in that same cave. His leg is injured. That's why he can't get out."

"And you know that because?" Ionescu asked.

She glanced at Roman and then back at the inspector. "I have a special connection with animals, an ability to communicate with them."

Ionescu leaned back in his chair. "You talk to animals?"

Philly straightened in hers. "Not usually in words. They sometimes send me images, colors, feelings. I've seen the rock ledge where Caliban is lying. And that fits with what Delos told Alexi—that he'd seen Caliban in one of the caves. I'm betting it was the cave Roman and I found the surveillance camera in. And when Delos came out, he was shot. And minutes after Roman and I came out, *we* were shot at. I'm betting the jewels Delos was looking for are in that cave, too."

"It's an interesting theory," Ionescu said.

"Well, why don't you go up to the Castello and check it out?"

"On the word of a woman who claims to be able to communicate with cats?"

Roman could see Philly's temper bubbling to the surface, so he put a hand on her arm and said, "When we leave here, Philly and I are flying to Athens. Gianni Stassis has sent his private plane. He's made arrangements for us to talk with Carlo Ferrante."

Ionescu set down his pen and leaned back in his chair. "You work fast, Mr. Oliver."

"When I'm properly motivated. By the way, I agree with everything Philly has said, and I think Andre Magellan is involved. If he didn't steal the jewels, he may be using this party to fence them."

"That's an interesting theory also."

"The cave we're talking about is at the foot of his estate, and according to Ariel there's a second, very convenient entrance to that cave right on the grounds of the Castello," Philly said.

"So you believe there is a second entrance because a cat has led you to believe it." Expressionless, Ionescu turned to Roman. "When will you return from Athens?"

"Tomorrow sometime. It will depend on exactly when we can meet with Mr. Ferrante."

"I'll be interested in the results of your meeting."

Philly leaned forward in her chair. "When are you going to release my cousin? Surely you must see that he's not behind these incidents. He was here with you when those men tried to kill us. You should be questioning Andre Magellan."

"I'll get around to that when I have more evidence."

"More evidence?" She began to tick items off on her fingers. "He has a security camera on one of his caves."

Ionescu shrugged. "There's no law against that."

"He ordered his men to shoot at Ariel. That's attempted murder."

"Of a cat."

"What about getting a warrant or whatever it is you have to get to search the grounds for the second entrance to the cave where Caliban is trapped? Surely you can do that."

Ionescu's brows shot up. "Ms. Angelis, even if I believed you—and I'm not a complete skeptic…my mother swears her father had the gift of clairvoyance—I can hardly force Andre Magellan to let me search his estate for a cat, especially on the eve of his party. All the people who would have to approve such a warrant will be attending the party. And if I go search the area where you were shot at, it may only alert the shooters that you are still alive.

I'd prefer to wait and see what you learn from Carlo Ferrante first."

"What about the two men who trapped us in that cave? They have to be working for Magellan."

Ionescu turned his hands over, palms up. "I don't have any proof of that."

Philly frowned. "And just what kind of proof do you have against my cousin?"

"The bullet that killed Antony Delos came from the gun we found in Alexi's room."

Philly whitened at the news. "He didn't do it. The shooter that I saw was high up near the Castello. Alexi wouldn't have had time to get all the way up there."

"I'm not so sure of that. He knows that cliff very well. He's been climbing it since he was a boy."

Philly shot out of her chair. "What's his motive? You surely don't suspect that he's involved in the jewel theft Mr. Delos was investigating?"

"I suspect many things, Ms. Angelis. One of them is that if Alexi is innocent, someone has gone to some trouble to frame him. Also, judging from your experience this afternoon, I think he's safer here than he would be running around searching those caves."

Recognizing the truth of that statement, Philly subsided and sank into her chair.

Ionescu shifted his gaze to Roman. "I had to work hard to convince Mr. Andros, the legal representative your Mr. Stassis sent, to see it my way. But he finally agreed. I've been seeing Miranda Kostas for the past year, so I've had some time to get to know Alexi. Miranda does her best, but he's a headstrong young man, and he's grown more so since his father died. And he's very close to those cats."

He returned his gaze to Philly. "I'm worried for your

safety, too, Ms. Angelis. You might consider spending the rest of your holiday in Athens instead of returning to Corfu."

"I can't leave Corfu until I find Caliban, and Alexi is out of jail."

Roman rose then and extended his hand to Ionescu. "Would it be possible for us to see Alexi before we leave? Miranda sent some food for him."

"Of course. One of my men will take you to him."

IT TWISTED MY HEART to see my cousin sitting in a cell, holding his head in his hands. I was very grateful that Miranda had been too busy with her guests to pay him a visit yet.

"Alexi?"

When he glanced up, he looked much younger and more vulnerable than the angry man I'd first seen arguing with Antony Delos on the beach. "We're your cousins, Philly and Kit, and we've brought something from your mother."

He rose immediately and came to the bars that caged him in. "How is she?"

"Worried," I said. "It helps that she's busy. How are you?"

"I want to get out of here." He turned to Roman. "Thank you for sending Mr. Andros to represent me. He said he was going to work on getting me out of here."

"He's still working on it."

For the first time I saw fire flash into Alexi's eyes. "I need to find Caliban. He's in one of the caves. Delos told me that much."

I saw then that Inspector Ionescu was right. If freed, Alexi was hotheaded enough to go back and search the caves beneath the Castello, one by one. And he'd meet the same fate that Delos had.

"Alexi," I said, "we believe that Antony Delos was killed

because he'd been looking through the caves for some stolen jewels. Do you know anything about them?"

"Jewels?" He ran a hand through his hair. "What are you talking about?"

Whatever doubts I may have harbored about my cousin vanished as I saw the complete bafflement on his face. I told him about what had happened to Roman and me that morning right after we'd come out of the cave where I thought Caliban was trapped.

"Ariel saved you?"

I explained to him about my ability to communicate with animals. He was more accepting of the possibility than Ionescu had been.

"Caliban's all right then?"

"For now." I wouldn't have agreed to go to Athens with Roman if I hadn't believed that.

Roman spoke for the first time. "You wouldn't be able to do anything more than you're doing right now. You've tried before to get inside the Castello grounds and failed. And if you got yourself killed, that wouldn't save Caliban."

Alexi met Roman's eyes and something passed between the two men. Silent guy talk. I'd seen the same looks pass between my brothers. Finally my cousin nodded. "Right. You're right."

"Philly and I have talked to Ionescu, and there's nothing he can do to help. He doesn't have anything he can use as a lever on Magellan to force his cooperation. But Philly and I are flying to Athens when we leave here. We hope to find that leverage before we return."

After a long moment, Alexi nodded again. "All right."

I had the satisfaction of seeing that he looked a great deal better as we left.

10

I'D NEVER FLOWN in a private jet before. I'd seen them in movies, of course. But Gianni Stassis's private jet was a definite step up from anything I'd seen or imagined. It boasted a bedroom, a bathroom with a shower and a galley that was about the same size as the kitchen in my apartment back in San Francisco. The main cabin had leather-covered sofas instead of regular airline seats.

The pilot had offered us a quick tour before takeoff. There was wine and a selection of food in the galley. We were to make ourselves completely at home. He'd indicated he expected to touch down at the Athens airport in about an hour.

I couldn't quite explain it, but enclosed in the small plane I felt somehow distanced from everything else that had happened that day.

I'd been too nervous—and too impressed—to help myself from the selections in the galley, but Roman seemed to take it all in stride. He'd poured himself some coffee and settled on one of the wide leather sofas.

I supposed that Oliver Enterprises had its own jet, too. There were a lot of things about Roman's life and his work that I knew nothing about—or hadn't thought about before.

He sat across from me, reading a file he'd taken from his briefcase. In the black slacks and white shirt he'd changed in to at the villa, he looked every inch the CEO. And he was totally caught up in what he'd spread out on the sofa. I'd noted his ability to focus completely on whatever held his attention at the moment many times before when I'd watched him play tennis or shoot pool with my brothers. The quality made him an excellent listener. And an extraordinary lover.

I was almost getting used to the little shiver of excitement that moved through me whenever I thought of making love with Roman. And I thought about it a lot. I recalled the quick, hot bout of sex we'd had in that cave, the desperation I'd felt in the press of his hands, in each thrust of his body.

How was I ever going to walk away from him once our stay in Greece was over? It had been hard enough before, thinking about him, wanting him, wondering how it might be. But now that I'd touched him, tasted him. Now that I knew what it was like to have him moving inside of me, how was I ever going to live without him?

The plane took a little lurch.

Roman's eyes met mine. "Are you all right?"

"Fine," I lied.

He went back to his file.

It occurred to me then, with the same clarity I'd experienced when I'd seen that white bird fly out of the Castello's tower, that I didn't have to live without Roman. The old Philly would. *She'd* given up in that hospital room the instant he'd fed her that line about his feelings for her being brotherly. She'd just walked out with a dent in her heart and wasted a whole month trying to forget him.

But he'd been lying.

Well, so had I. Everything I'd told him at dinner last night—that I only wanted an affair, one that would end once we left Corfu—was a total crock. I was just as big a liar as he was. I'd always wanted more than an affair with Roman.

The difference was that the old Philly would have made do without what she really wanted. But not the new Philly—not the Philly I'd become since I'd made love with Roman Oliver. The Fates had brought us together here in Greece, and I was going to take everything they were offering and maybe more—whether Roman liked it or not.

Roman met my eyes then. "You're distracting me."

"From what?" I smiled at him.

He set his pen down and rubbed the back of his neck. "I mentioned at dinner last night that Gianni Stassis and Oliver Enterprises are negotiating an agreement to invest in a select group of small hotels in Greece—both on the mainland and on the islands. We're not looking to buy or develop new properties at first, but if we work well together, our business plan will expand."

"You said at dinner that the Villa Prospero is a good example of the kind of hotel you'd be approaching."

He nodded. "It's small, family operated and it has a great location. It's filled to capacity right now because of the party at the Castello Corli, but according to Demetria, they're often only booked at around seventy percent. If Miranda is willing to sell us part interest, Oliver–Stassis could offer her ways to cut her workload and increase her profits. If Stassis and I can come to terms, I intend to approach Miranda."

"What will you offer her?"

"Right now, the Villa Prospero is very low-tech. One of the first things that Oliver–Stassis would do would be to nudge the operation into the twenty-first century. It doesn't even have a Web site. I was thinking that Alexi might very well become more interested in the family hotel if he were able to participate in that side of the business—depending on what he's capable of."

I thought he might be very right. "You've been very busy. This will be your first venture out of the States, right?"

"Yes."

"Why did you choose Greece?"

Roman's smile held a hint of ruefulness. "My father asked the same question. He wanted to know if I was thinking of taking the company global why I hadn't chosen Italy. But your father had been singing the praises of Greece ever since he made that trip a little over a year ago and brought back Helena."

That was certainly true. Everyone who'd sat at the bar of the Poseidon during the past year had gotten an earful of how great my dad's trip to Greece was, and he'd added even more stories since he and Helena had honeymooned there.

"It was Helena who actually mentioned Gianni Stassis to me. He owned the five-star restaurant where she was the head chef, and he dined there frequently when he was in Athens. She mentioned that he'd come into the kitchen each time he was there to compliment her on the dishes she'd prepared."

"So he's a man who likes to keep in personal contact with his investments," I observed.

"And he values and treats his employees well when they do a good job."

I imagined that Roman oversaw his own business ventures with the same care.

Roman sipped coffee. "It was your aunt Cass who gave me the final push. About a month ago, right after I got out of the hospital, she came to my office and told me she'd seen something in her crystals about a business opportunity in Greece."

"Aunt Cass does readings for you?" That was something I didn't know.

Roman shook his head. "No. I was surprised that she came to me. But I've known your family too long not to have great respect for the work she does. Besides, I'd had this idea playing around in the back of my head for a while. So I did some research on Gianni Stassis and made a phone call. The bottom line is that I like him. All three of your brothers checked him out for me, and he seems to have a Midas touch when it comes to business ventures."

I raised my eyebrows. "And Oliver Enterprises doesn't?"

"We do when the chief negotiator is prepared." He gestured toward the files spread out on the table. "I'm sure Stassis will want to discuss business at some point. I've already postponed him twice."

I couldn't say that I felt sorry for keeping Roman from his business. In fact, the idea that I could distract him thrilled me.

"Sorry," I lied. The old Philly would have meant it and shut up. But I found that I was enjoying being the new Philly and I was enjoying talking to Roman. In the seven years that we'd known each other, we'd seldom conversed one-on-one.

"What did my brother Kit tell you when he phoned?" Kit had called Roman's cell during the ride to the airport. I'd spoken with him briefly, and he'd done the brotherly thing with me—was I all right? Was I behaving myself? But then he'd talked to Roman until we'd arrived at the airport. "He dug up some stuff on Carlo Ferrante and Andre Magellan, right?"

Roman rubbed his eyes, then leaned back against the leather couch. "The two of them have a history that dates back to their college days at Oxford. They were supposedly best friends, but they were always in competition with one another. According to Kit, the men might as well be clones of one another. Both come from money—scads of it. The Magellan family made its money in banking while the Ferrantes made their fortune in shipping. In spite of the fact that they're both in their midthirties, neither has worked even one day for their family's respective businesses."

"What do they do?"

"That's the only thing they seem to differ on. Magellan lives the extravagant life of a playboy. He usually has a significant piece of eye candy on his arm. Ferrante, on the other hand, leads a more reclusive life. He raises horses and makes a nice profit on that little sideline. He's rarely seen in public and doesn't have the womanizing reputation that Magellan does. They each have a penchant for collecting things that only the rich can afford—rare artifacts, priceless paintings, jewels, estates. Curiously enough, Kit says that whenever one of them acquires a new house, the other follows suit within months. When Magellan's parents gave him the Castello Corli, Ferrante picked up a medieval castle in Scotland."

"They're still rivals?"

"It would seem so, but they're no longer friends. Something happened their junior year at Oxford. Kit hasn't been able to get the full story yet—only that they both kept horses at a nearby stable, and the falling-out occurred after Ferrante's horse broke his leg and Ferrante had to shoot him. After that, their days at Oxford were marked by bitter rivalry."

"Interesting. Then this robbery may have personal implications."

"And the jewels have been stolen twice now. That's got to gall the hell out of Ferrante—especially if Magellan was behind both thefts. Kit's still digging into the museum heist and the mysterious return of the jewels. And he thinks there was more to their falling-out than a horse. He's tracking down a lead that has to do with a woman. Stassis put some investigators on it also, so we may know more after we get to his yacht."

For a moment, silence stretched between us, and we continued to look at each other. The air in the cabin seemed to grow thicker, the space smaller. All he had to do was look at me, and I wanted him. It was just that elemental. I was revving up the courage to say, "Want to fool around?" or something equally corny, when Roman said, "Why don't you take a nap while I finish with this file."

Talk about a dash of cold water!

He shifted his gaze to his briefcase, reached in and pulled out a pair of reading glasses. When he put them on, I was hit by a wave of pure lust. I hadn't thought Roman could look any sexier, but I was dead wrong.

Take a nap? Not a chance.

Something impish and reckless moved through me. In terms of how we were going to spend the rest of the time on our short flight to Athens, Roman and I had reached an impasse of sorts. He wanted to work and I—didn't. I recalled how he'd convinced me to come to Athens by telling me that sometimes what one needed to solve a problem was a different approach. I had one in mind.

I stretched, taking my time. Then I rose and idly walked toward the galley. I was wearing slacks, too, and I'd paid a week's worth of pet-consulting fees for the designer fit. Even with my back turned, I knew the instant his eyes skimmed over me. Every inch of my skin heated.

Halfway to the galley, I stepped out of one of my shoes, then the other. Pausing in the doorway, I took my time selecting a strawberry and then I turned back toward Roman.

He was watching me now, and I held his gaze for five pulsing seconds before I bit into the fruit.

This time he didn't go back to the file. Feeling like Eve, I held the half-eaten fruit out. "Want a bite?"

"What are you doing?"

"Watch." Encouraged by the ragged edge to his voice, I put the strawberry down and began to unbutton my blouse.

When it slid to the floor, he said, "Philly…"

"Hmm?" I stretched again, lifting my arms over my head, then slowly lowered them to unfasten my belt.

Roman didn't speak again, but his eyes had shifted to my hands. I'd never stripped for anyone before, never even fantasized about it, so I was surprised to find that I was arousing myself as much as I was hopefully arousing Roman. I pulled the belt slowly from its loops and dropped it.

The button at the waist of my slacks came next. As I freed it, fire licked along my nerve endings and my heart raced. The zipper made an erotic sound in the stillness of the cabin.

WHAT WAS SHE DOING to him? He'd vowed to himself that he wasn't going to touch her on the plane trip to Athens. She'd had a roller coaster of a day both physically and emotionally. They'd been shot at, and had escaped from a narrow cave that would have challenged even the great Houdini's skills. And seeing her cousin in that cell had taken its toll on her.

But when the slacks hit the floor and she stood in the doorway to the galley wearing nothing but wisps of white lace, he heard something deep inside of him snap. It shouldn't have. He'd never encountered another woman who could shred his resolve this way. But all Philly had to do was smile and crook her finger at him, and he was helpless to prevent himself from rising and striding toward her.

When he grabbed her shoulders, pushing her far enough into the galley to shut the door, her throaty laugh shot his blood well past the boiling point.

"Want something to eat?" she asked.

"You know what I want."

She rose on her toes and touched her mouth to his chin. "I think I do."

"I promised myself I wasn't going to do this." But his hands were racing over her while he rained kisses on her eyelids, her cheekbones. "You should rest."

"You know what they say about no rest for the wicked. And you make me feel very, very wicked." She pulled his shirt out of his trousers and slid her hands beneath it. Her fingers sent tremors running along every nerve ending.

Drawing in a deep breath, Roman fastened his hands at her hips and set her away from him—or at least as far as he could in the cramped space. When she was standing at the far wall of the galley, he backed against the door. Even then, they were less than five feet apart. He took another breath. If he didn't slow down, he was going to take her like a madman. His usual technique with Philly, it seemed.

She was still wearing a bra, a thong and those lace-topped stockings she seemed to favor. "Finish what you started. Take the rest off."

She slipped the bra off first, twirling it around her finger before she dropped it to the floor. The sight of her nipples—tight and red as raspberries—had his mouth watering. He kept himself from reaching out only by putting his hands behind his back and gripping the handle of the door.

She moved her hands to the first stocking. It gave him some satisfaction to see her fingers tremble as she slid them beneath the band of lace and then slowly rolled it down her leg.

The movement was more than enough to have his control slipping again. Dropping to his knees, he took care of the second one himself, tracing its path downward with his mouth. The stockings were sheer and shades lighter than the creamy smooth skin they covered. Removing them was like unwrapping a present. He took his time, lingering on the softness of her inner thigh, enjoying the scent at the back of her knee, nipping her ankle. When the bit of lace and silk was finally off, he lifted her foot, and easing back so that he could see her face, he licked and kissed each one of her toes. Her eyes went beyond dark to opaque.

"I love your taste," he murmured, pressing one last kiss to the sole of her foot before he set it on the floor. Then using teeth and tongue, he journeyed back up to where a lacy, white thong still covered that most intimate part of her. He lowered it, keeping his eyes on hers. Her hands were gripping the counters on either side, and her knuckles had gone white.

"I have to taste you here, Philly." He spread her thighs and used his thumbs to part her folds. Finally, he leaned forward and feasted. Her flavors streaked through him, each darker, more secret and more dangerous than the last. When she arched toward him and cried out his name on a ragged breath, he continued to ply his tongue on her until she rode out the climax.

Still on his knees, Roman drew back and watched his own hands tremble as he dealt with his trousers and the condom. There was only one thought in his head. He had to be inside of her. He had to lose himself in that wet heat. He glanced around, but the space was cramped and everywhere he looked there were sharp edges—the counters, even the door.

"Roman, I want you."

"Working on it." He gripped her hips and turned her round, then as he inched his way backward, he pulled her down so that the were both kneeling and facing the back wall of the galley.

"Let's try this."

I DID WHAT HE ASKED as I felt his erection pressing against me, hot and hard. But it wasn't quite in the right spot. Pushing against the side of the plane, I tried to wiggle backward. In one smooth movement, Roman filled me.

I gasped. The pressure was huge, the angle so different.

"Are you all right?"

I wiggled again, pressing myself back against him. "I will be once you start moving."

His hands tightened on my hips. "I'm going to try to go slowly." As if to demonstrate, he pulled almost all the way out of me, then pushed back in. This time he seemed to sink even deeper.

"No promises," he said.

I didn't want any. "Just don't stop."

He didn't. But he kept the rhythm slow. Too slow. Each time he withdrew, he left an aching emptiness behind. And each time he thrust in, he increased the incredible pressure building inside of me. But it wasn't enough.

"Go faster," I demanded.

"Soon," he promised and sank his teeth into my shoulder. Pleasure and pain spiraled through me. "Roman, please."

"You were teasing me before. I'm just returning the favor. How about this?" He moved one of his hands to cover my breast. "Does this help?"

"No." But when he used his thumb and forefinger to pinch my nipple, I cried out, and the first wave of my climax moved through me.

He began to move faster then, and harder.

My first climax had barely subsided before the second one slammed into me, carrying me into a tight dark world that shattered around me.

11

"MS. ANGELIS." Gianni Stassis raised my hand to his lips. "Would you mind terribly if Roman and I leave you alone for a short while?"

"No. Not at all." After giving us a tour of his yacht, Gianni had invited us to enjoy iced coffee and a selection of fruit and cheese on the aft deck.

"I'm sure you would be bored with our business discussion. And we won't be too long. I'm expecting Carlo Ferrante shortly. If you want anything, just press the button for my man, Kyros. He takes care of all my guests' needs, and he's standing by."

"I'm fine," I assured him. "I could stand here for hours and just enjoy the view."

When he and Roman had left to go belowdecks, I did just that. I'd been impressed with Gianni Stassis's jet, but I was overwhelmed by the luxury of his yacht. It occurred to me as I stood at the railing watching the late-afternoon sun shoot blinding sparks of light off the Mediterranean Sea that I'd met a genuine Greek tycoon. And he was charming. No wonder Helena had been impressed and I could see why Roman liked him. I did, too.

From the airport in Athens, we'd boarded a waiting helicopter that had set us down at the edge of the harbor where Gianni's yacht, the *Alexander,* was moored. Kyros, who I figured was a sort of a butler, had met us and ferried us to the yacht. I guessed Gianni's age to be somewhere in his late thirties—young for a tycoon. He was dressed casually in khaki slacks and an open-necked knit shirt, and wore his almost black hair pulled back into a ponytail. While he wasn't handsome in a movie-star kind of way, Gianni Stassis had a way of smiling that would make a woman forget that.

He also had the same kind of focus on business that Roman had. It had only taken him fifteen minutes before he'd whisked Roman away, and Roman hadn't made any objection.

I didn't mind at all. In fact, I welcomed a chance to just be alone. Being with Roman had a strange effect on my brain cells, not to mention my body. Following our session of hot sweaty sex in the galley, Roman and I had showered together, made love again and still managed to dress and get into our seats before the copilot had entered the cabin to tell us that we were about to land. The moment the man had returned to the cockpit, Roman had whispered, "Perfect timing." Then we'd both laughed like idiots as the plane had bumped down on the Athens runway.

A fishing boat cut across our prow heading out to sea. I waved and one of the men on deck waved back. We weren't actually moored in Athens, but just below the city along the Attica coast. So the ruins of the temple I was looking at high on a hill to my right wasn't the Acropolis, which we'd flown over in the helicopter.

To my mind it was close enough. Looking at those ancient, larger-than-life columns shooting up into the clear blue sky reminded me of the Greece I'd studied in textbooks. And Gianni had said that if we had time for a sail tomorrow he'd take us to see the ruins of the Temple of

Poseidon. I wondered if Roman had mentioned my family's restaurant in San Francisco, or if Gianni Stassis had run a background check on me once he'd learned that I'd be coming with Roman. I'd bet on the latter. He'd impressed me as a thorough man; I thought he and Roman would make good business partners.

Closer to the harbor, more fishing boats were anchored. My father's father had been a fisherman, and my brothers and father still were drawn to the sea. I was also, mostly when I needed to clear my mind and think. Which is exactly what I needed to do right now.

Leaning against the railing, I let my mind return to our frantic search of the caves that morning. We hadn't had time to check all of them, but I was still banking on the theory I'd proposed to Inspector Ionescu—that Caliban was trapped in the cave with the surveillance camera. It was too bad that I hadn't been able to establish a link with him. But some animals were more open to communication than others. My own Pretzels was much more communicative than his sister, Peanuts.

Roman and I might not ever have wandered into that cave—we might never have discovered the camera if it hadn't been for the storm. Providence? Fate? You couldn't be an Angelis and not believe in both.

The way I figured it, Magellan had to be the person watching that particular cave. It just made sense. The cave was on Magellan's property. Who else would have equipped it with a camera if not him?

Everything pointed to the fact that Magellan wanted to keep people away from that cave. I thought of the angry encounter he'd had with Miranda and how adamant he'd been that Alexi and his cats keep away from the caves and his estate. The question was why, and the answer had to be the stolen jewels. And the man had quite a temper. If he'd come across Caliban in the cave where he'd hidden the jewels, he was fully capable of striking out in irritation and injuring him with the butt of a gun. After all, I'd seen him order his men to shoot at Ariel.

Then there was Delos. He'd been hot on the trail of the stolen jewels, and he'd come upon the cave that Caliban was in. He'd told Alexi that much. And Delos had also found something in one of the caves that had sent him hightailing it back to the Villa Prospero to make a phone call.

Killing him and framing Alexi for the shooting had been a great way to eliminate two people who were poking around that cave. Excitement prickled along my skin. I still didn't have what Ionescu would call evidence, but my theory was more coherent. I wanted to talk to Roman about it. No, I *needed* to talk to Roman about it.

Before I'd come to Greece, I'd been too shy, too aware of my attraction to him, too hung up to talk with Roman about much of anything. Now I wanted to talk to him about everything. My heart didn't just drop this time. It took a huge bounce.

What if Roman didn't feel the same way?

Ripples of fear moved through me, but I ruthlessly shoved them down. If Roman didn't feel the same way I did, I would just have to convince him otherwise. No way was I going to give up as I had in his hospital room.

Suddenly, my attention was snagged by a seaplane making a neat landing about fifty feet off the prow of the yacht. Within moments, it had been met by a small boat, and a man climbed aboard. The man, a tall broad-shouldered figure wearing black sunglasses, black slacks and a black T-shirt, carried a small dog in his arms. I guessed he was Carlo Ferrante. The man piloting the boat docked and pulled out the stairs so that Carlo could board the yacht.

When he stepped onto the deck and saw me, he moved immediately in my direction. He carried the dog securely tucked under one arm. I was sensing a bubbly, happy female, and she was curious about me. I couldn't place the breed, but she had the size and look of a Havanese or a shih tzu.

"Ms. Angelis?" he asked as he reached me.

"Yes."

"Carlo Ferrante." He smiled as he held out a hand. "It's a pleasure."

I studied him as I shook his hand. The smile was as powerful as Gianni's, but Carlo Ferrante also possessed movie-star good looks. He reminded me a little of Antonio Banderas. I found the contrast of large man and small dog intriguing.

She chose that moment to speak to me. *I'm Gemma.*

"Gemma is a pretty name." I spoke aloud so that Carlo Ferrante could hear. "I'm Philly."

Carlo frowned. "How do you know her name?"

"She told me. I have an ability to communicate with animals. In San Francisco, I work part-time in a veterinary hospital and as a pet psychic."

"Yes, I learned about your business when I checked you out. The photo on your Web site is a very good likeness."

The dog began to wiggle in Carlo's arms, and when I held mine out, she scrambled into them and began to lick my face. "You probably thought it was all a scam."

He took his sunglasses off, and for the first time I saw his eyes. There was a hardness there, but it softened as he shifted his gaze to Gemma. "The thought did occur to me. She doesn't usually take so easily to strangers."

Gemma had settled, snuggling into the crook of my arm.

"So what is it exactly you do in your pet-psychic business, Ms. Angelis?"

"Most of my clients are referrals from the veterinarian I work for. Frequently, the animals are having some problem that isn't medical, and they want to solve it. When a session goes well, the animal can tell me what's bothering them."

"Just like that?" His tone was laced with skepticism, something that I ran into all the time—even from prospective clients. "Perhaps you discovered Gemma's name when your friend Roman Oliver ran a background check on me."

I met his eyes squarely. A man who valued his privacy the way I suspected Carlo Ferrante did wouldn't like the fact that someone had been able to probe that closely. "Perhaps I could have, but I didn't. Would you like me to ask Gemma if she has any problems?"

"A little test?" This time I heard curiosity in his tone. "Go ahead. She doesn't have any that I'm aware of."

I cleared my mind as I scratched Gemma under her chin. *Is there anything that's bothering you, Gemma girl?*

I received a vivid picture of food in a fancy china bowl.

"There's something about what you're feeding her that she doesn't like," I relayed to Carlo.

He frowned then. "I have my chef prepare it. But he did tell me that she's been turning her nose up at it lately."

"Have him experiment until he finds something she likes."

He glanced at Gemma, then back at me. "You couldn't have known that from any kind of background check. Henri only mentioned it to me this morning. It's been going on for a week, and he was worried. Is there anything else bothering her?"

I sensed that he was a man who sincerely loved animals, and that did a lot to gain my admiration. *Gemma, are you worried about anything else?*

An image flashed into my mind. Carlo Ferrante standing in a stable, his hand on a huge black stallion.

"It's not about Gemma," I told Carlo. "She's sending me an image of a horse—a black stallion."

Carlo frowned. "Lucifer. He's off his feed, too. He has been ever since his barn cat passed on. They'd been together since he was a colt."

"Since I'm not communicating with Lucifer directly, I can't say for sure what the problem is. But you might want to try getting him a new barn cat. He may be missing the companionship."

Carlo's eyes had narrowed. "You surprise me, Ms. Angelis. People rarely do."

I bet they didn't.

"What do I owe you for your services?"

I smiled at him. "This wasn't a consultation. It was a test, remember?"

"Ah, yes."

"Did I pass it?" Gemma had begun to snore on my shoulder.

He glanced at her and murmured, "With flying colors. If I wanted a consultation, could I send my private jet to fly you to Tuscany?"

My eyes widened a bit at that. "As lovely as that sounds, you wouldn't have to. All you'd have to do is pick up a phone and call me. The animal has to be near you, but I can do consultations over the phone as successfully as in person."

"If I can't pay you, I owe you a favor. I've been very worried about Lucifer."

A favor from a billionaire and I was on the yacht of a Greek tycoon. It occurred to me that I was traveling in very rarefied circles.

"Carlo." A voice from behind Carlo had us both turning

to see Gianni and Roman climb up on deck. "Roman and I were discussing business and my man Kyros didn't tell us of your arrival."

"That's my fault," I apologized. "I didn't ring for Kyros when Mr. Ferrante boarded."

Looking toward me, he said, "Call me Carlo, please."

"If I call you Carlo, you must call me Philly."

"Philly then."

As he, Gianni and Roman went through the ritual of shaking hands, he continued, "And I must claim full responsibility for the delay in announcing my arrival. I was doing a pet consultation with Philly."

"I know we're all pressed for time," Gianni said, "so why don't we go below and discuss our business." Turning, he led the way.

Roman took my arm, easing me back from the other two men. "You're making quite an impression on Gianni and Carlo."

There was more than a trace of annoyance in his voice, so I studied him for a moment. Then it dawned on me that he was jealous. That had to be a good sign, and I couldn't prevent a little thrill from moving through me. "They're both very charming men."

"And ruthless as hell. I can handle Gianni, but don't let Ferrante fool you just because he likes animals. Gianni just warned me that Ferrante has the reputation of being a user. He'll use both of us and not mind the consequences to get what he wants. I'm considering canceling this meeting and taking you back to Corfu."

I stiffened then. "Whoa." I fisted my hands on my hips. "You're not taking me anywhere. And just what would we do back in Corfu anyway? Remember the impasse we've reached? You're the one who said we needed to explore taking a different approach. I'm not leaving until we find out what Carlo has to tell us about his old school chum, Andre Magellan."

"Fine."

But as we hurried to catch up with Gianni and Carlo, the new Philly was thrilled to realize that he didn't sound fine at all.

12

GIANNI STASSIS LED us into a state-of-the-art conference room. There were several flat computer screens nearly covering one wall that I supposed were for videoconferencing. Two of the other walls were paneled in a dark wood and lined with bookshelves and cabinets. The fourth wall was made of glass and offered a view of the sea all the way to the horizon.

Kyros was pouring coffee and setting glasses of ice water at four places. Still holding the sleeping Gemma, I took the chair next to Roman and we faced the two men across a gleaming table of inlaid wood.

"What can you tell me about what's going on at the Castello Corli?" Carlo asked.

Roman raised a hand. "Not so fast. I asked Gianni to arrange this meeting so that you could tell me what you know about Andre Magellan and the theft of your jewels, so let's begin with that."

Carlo's lips curved slightly, but the smile didn't reach his eyes. "Gianni warned me that you were a tough negotiator. You probably already know some of it. Andre and I went to school together at Oxford."

"You were friends," Roman said. "What caused you to have a falling-out?"

Carlo's eyebrows rose. "You have done your homework.

Andre was responsible for the death of my horse, Michelangelo. We were having a race. Even when we were close friends, Andre always wanted to have some sort of competition. If I were a psychologist, I would say that he has a fundamental need to prove himself superior to anyone else. He would frequently challenge me to a horse race, and usually I won—Michelangelo was an extraordinary horse. This particular day, I should have suspected something as soon as I mounted him. He was jittery. And he reared up twice trying to throw me off before we started. It was when we got to the first jump that it happened. His front leg hit the fence, and he went over hard, tossing me and breaking his leg. I had to have him put down. The vet told me that it hadn't been an accident, that someone had put a steel burr beneath Michelangelo's blanket, and it had been digging deeper and deeper into him as we rode."

"Andre Magellan did that to your horse?" I asked.

"I couldn't prove it. But he did it. I vowed revenge." There was a coldness in his tone that had a sliver of ice shooting up my spine.

"Have you gotten it?" Roman asked.

Carlo smiled that frigid smile of his once more. "Not yet. But I will. I want it to be thorough and irrevocable."

I recalled Roman saying that Magellan and Ferrante could be clones of one another, and for the first time I was beginning to see that possibility. But Ferrante was more self-contained. I couldn't help but think that made Carlo Ferrante the more dangerous of the two.

"How did he get his hands on your jewels?" I asked.

Carlo hesitated for a moment, and his gaze shifted to Gemma who was still sleeping comfortably in my arms. That seemed to decide him. "I'm going to tell you more than I intended. Andre Magellan is a very rich man, but not because of his family's money. They cut most of it off years ago when they realized he'd never work in the family business. No, he runs a very lucrative side venture fencing stolen property. He stores the booty—sometimes artwork, sometimes priceless artifacts, often jewels—in an old smugglers' cave that runs from the sea to one of the towers of the old fortress. The parties he throws serve as a cover for his transactions. Among the guests will be several collectors who are there to bid on the jewels. The bidding goes on at the party. It's a silent auction. Magellan takes the bids on small pieces of paper that selected guests pass him as he makes his way among them. It's all done very discreetly. No one knows who else is bidding or what the actual bids are. The prize goes to the highest bidder."

"Wouldn't he get higher bids if he allowed the bidding to be competitive?" I asked.

"On the contrary," Ferrante replied, "if you only have one chance to get whatever it is he's selling, you tend to put in a very high bid in an attempt to win. The money is exchanged via electronic transfer from one numbered account to another. So there's no paperwork, no money trail. Then the winner will be escorted down to the cave to collect his newly purchased property."

"You're very familiar with his operation," Roman commented.

"I should be. Five years ago I was one of the bidders."

"Five years ago," Roman said. "That would have been just after your family jewels were stolen from the museum in Belgium. So this is the second time he's taken your jewels."

There were three beats before Carlo Ferrante answered. "I'm impressed, Mr. Oliver. But you're absolutely right. He was behind the museum robbery, and to rub salt in the wound, I received an invitation to his annual party at the Castello Corli. I was allowed to bid on my own jewels. And I lost. I expected to. But Andre offered me a tour of the smugglers' cave. He wanted me to see the jewels I wasn't going to get. I stored every detail away, and I even sketched some maps of the cave. It's quite large and is lined with rock ledges along the walls. Rainwater enters the cave from someplace above and the walls are always slick and damp. It's impossible to climb them. I tried."

I shot Roman a glance. What Carlo Ferrante was describing fit the images that Ariel had been sending me of Caliban. He had to be near the top of the cave. But Roman never took his eyes off of Ferrante. I noted that Gianni was watching the two men very carefully.

"There's a rope ladder you have to climb down from the opening near the tower. That's what we used to enter the cave. My jewels were wedged securely behind some rocks on the right wall. That way, they were protected from the tide that nearly fills the cave each time it comes in. It was while I was looking at the jewels and inspecting the recess that he hit me over the head and left me to die."

I gasped. Roman made no sound whatsoever.

"Fortunately, he'd only stunned me, so I pretended to be unconscious while he climbed back up the rope ladder. Then I discovered he'd taken it with him. The tide was already around my ankles and I wasted precious moments trying to climb up the rock ledges. Finally, I decided to try my luck with the entrance to the cave. It was a battle, but I made it out, then almost died making my way along the cliff face to the beach. The waves were nearly up to my waist by that time, and each one nearly dragged me out to sea. Of course, I took the jewels with me. And I've had them until he stole them from my Tuscany villa a week ago."

"You wanted him to steal the jewels again, didn't you?" Roman asked.

Carlo's eyes sharpened on Roman.

"It only makes sense that you let him steal the jewels. You don't impress me as a man who wouldn't protect his possessions—especially after they'd been taken from you once before."

"You're very perceptive." He shifted his gaze to Gianni. "Be careful in your negotiations with this man." Carlo lifted his cup of coffee, took a sip, then leaned back in his chair. "I made him wait five years and then yes, I allowed him to steal my jewels back. Not that he did it personally. He works with a very fine craftsman who's never been caught or even charged."

"How did you set it up so that he wouldn't be suspicious?" Roman asked.

"Very carefully. Andre is not stupid. The man who stole them had to work hard to establish a relationship with one of my servants. She eventually gave the floor plans and the alarm codes to him. She played her part very well, and I've rewarded her appropriately."

"Then you sent Delos to get the jewels back?" I asked.

"Oh, no, my dear. I hired Delos to confirm the location and to inform both me and Interpol. I wanted to make sure that Andre was still using the cave. But Delos was killed before he could confirm anything. I wanted Andre to be caught on the night of the party, so he could be charged with the theft. I intended to put a permanent end to his little side business."

"There's a surveillance camera on the cliff-side entrance to the cave," I said.

"Ah. That's some indication that he's still using it." Carlo took another sip of coffee. "Now I think it's your turn to share information. What is your interest in my jewels?"

"We're not interested in them," I said. "We believe that one of my cousin's cats is lying injured on a rock ledge in one of the caves. We know that Delos saw him, but he was in a hurry to get back to the hotel—probably to inform you and Interpol of his discovery."

Then I told him everything from the moment I met Ariel, including the fact that my cousin was suspected of shooting Delos. I even told him about our harrowing escape up the tunnel-like cave.

Beneath the table, Roman pressed one of his feet down on mine. I took it to mean that I was giving Ferrante too much information. So I shut up.

Carlo tapped the fingers of one manicured hand on the table. "It sounds as though the jewels are still in that smugglers' cave and that Andre is determined to keep everyone away until after the party. If he came across the cats on one of his visits, he wouldn't have liked it. Now the search for the injured cat is bringing too much attention to his hiding place."

For a few moments there was silence in the room. "So you want to rescue the cat Caliban and clear your cousin, and I want Andre to be caught with my jewels and his fencing operation exposed. Perhaps there's a way that we can both achieve our goals."

Roman frowned. "How's that?"

"I have a very distant cousin, Princess Melina Rinaldi, who received an invitation to Andre's party. She's going to bid on the jewels and gather evidence of what Andre is really doing at these parties. And then she'll turn the information over to Interpol."

Carlo met my eyes directly. "You look very like her. The hair and eye color is different, but that could be easily remedied. And getting you a proper wardrobe would be no problem."

"What are you suggesting?" Roman asked.

"I'm offering Philly a chance to get on the grounds of the Castello Corli as one of the invited guests. She should easily be able to rescue the injured cat. If she gathers evidence and recovers my jewels in the process, that will be a bonus for me, and she will have the satisfaction of putting the man who tried to kill her—and you—behind bars."

"No way," Roman said. "It's too dangerous."

I turned to Roman. Logic was what I would need to convince him. "It's a foolproof way to get on the grounds. If we smuggle Ariel in with us, she'll lead us to the entrance of the cave. She knows just where Caliban is. And if we can find evidence that Magellan is running a fencing operation and had Delos killed, then Alexi will go free."

"It shouldn't be difficult to rescue him," Ferrante said. "He must be on a rock ledge fairly close to the tower entrance. Otherwise the tide would have gotten him."

"It shouldn't take long then," I said to Roman.

"I don't like it, Philly, and I won't allow you to go to that party alone."

"You could go with her," Carlo said. "Melina always travels with a bodyguard. You'd be at her side every minute."

I kept my eyes steady on Roman's. "This is what we came to Athens to discover—an alternate strategy."

Roman turned to Carlo. "Has Andre ever met your cousin before?"

"Never," Carlo said. "And she's a lot like me. She normally doesn't go to parties. She hasn't been photographed in public in years."

"But he's expecting her to bid on the jewels."

"Yes. That's what got her the invitation."

"Does he have any idea she's related to you?" Roman pressed.

"No. I'm not a careless man, and I have an affection for Melina. Besides, the connection is so distant that even the princess and I sometimes question its validity."

"It's a good plan," I said to Roman.

"It's risky as hell." He turned to Carlo and his voice was clipped and frosty. "We'll need backup from the local police."

Ferrante frowned. "We can't be sure that they're not in Magellan's pocket."

"I can assure you that Inspector Ionescu is just waiting to get some hard evidence on Magellan. You'll have to call him and tell him much of what you told us."

Ferrante considered for a moment, then said, "I'll have Delos's contact at Interpol call him."

"Okay, then we'll go forward with the masquerade." As Roman turned to me, he looked like a man caught between a rock and a hard place. "But at the first sign of trouble, we're getting off the grounds whether we have Caliban or not. Agreed?"

Since I couldn't see that happening, I agreed.

"She makes a beautiful princess, does she not?"

"Yes." Roman shifted his gaze from Gianni Stassis to the mirror that ran the length of the wall in front of him. Philly was clearly visible five chairs down and behind him. Currently, she was receiving a pedicure.

The last place he'd expected to spend the evening in Athens was in a beauty salon. Since the place was one of Stassis's many diverse business interests, they'd had no problem staying open after nine to work on the owner's friends. Neither had the boutique they'd just come from where Carlo Ferrante had supervised the selection of several outfits for the fake princess's wardrobe. Stassis had also arranged for the tuxedo Roman would wear to the party.

Philly had enjoyed the shopping spree. Roman hadn't. He didn't care for the proprietary attitude Ferrante had developed toward Philly. He'd cared for it even less when he'd realized the hard, painful knot in his stomach was jealousy.

No woman had ever made him jealous before, but Philly seemed to have a knack for it.

"What do you think, sir?"

Roman glanced at the hairdresser who'd been working on him, then shifted his attention back to his own image in the mirror. He'd refused Ferrante's suggestion that he lighten the color of his hair. Although there was no way to tell how digitally accurate the pictures captured by the surveillance cameras were, Roman was betting that the storm and the darkness of the cave would keep Andre Magellan from recognizing him. But he had agreed to let Josef change his hairstyle, giving it a more severe look. Roman had to admit Carlo had been right. The image in the mirror looked tougher. More like a bodyguard.

"It's excellent," Roman said.

"Yes," Gianni agreed. "You do look rather intimidating."

"Maybe I'll wear this new look at board meetings."

Gianni threw back his head and laughed. While Josef brushed off his clothes and cleaned up his work space, Roman turned his attention back to Philly. Doni, the head designer of the salon, had transformed her with the help of hair dye and contact lenses, into a blue-eyed blonde. The change was playing havoc with his libido and had lust warring uncomfortably with jealousy. Carlo Ferrante stood near Philly stroking Gemma while they chatted.

Roman just didn't like the man. More than that, he didn't trust him. His mind kept circling back to Kit's assessment that Ferrante and Magellan were as alike as two peas in a pod. How much of what Ferrante had told them about the jewels and the silent auction was the truth?

On the other hand, Roman had a great deal of respect for Gianni Stassis. The moment Josef was out of earshot, he spoke in a low tone to Stassis. "You've gone to a great deal of trouble. What's in all of this for you?"

Gianni met his eyes. "I want to do business with you. I believe that we can make a great deal of money together. It's also to my advantage to have a man like Carlo Ferrante in my debt."

"What would you say if I told you I don't trust him?"

Gianni spoke very softly. "I'd say what I already know about you. You're a very intelligent man, and a good judge of character."

Having Gianni agree with him wasn't making Roman feel any better.

"Do you know of anything other than the death of his horse that has fueled this intense rivalry Ferrante has with Magellan?"

"My private-investigative firm is still digging. There were rumors about a woman Magellan was dating around the same time. She died in a tragic car crash, and there was speculation that Ferrante had something to do with it—to get revenge." Gianni shrugged. "But it turned out to be nothing more than gossip. If Magellan suspected something like that, he would have gone to the police, and he didn't. The woman's death was judged to be accidental."

"Have you ever done business with him?" Roman asked.

"Once." Stassis's tone said *never again*.

"How did you persuade him to meet with Philly and me?"

"It wasn't difficult. I assume he was curious about what you knew concerning his jewels. And he wants to do business again with me. If I were you," Gianni continued, "I'd go into that party with a couple of backup plans in mind."

Shit, Roman thought. He was going to need more than a backup plan. He was going to need real backup. Rising from his chair, he said, "Could you keep Ferrante occupied for a few minutes? I need to make a phone call."

"What is it you Americans always say? No problem." Gianni moved down to Philly's station.

Walking toward the front of the salon, Roman decided that he was liking Gianni Stassis more and more. He was not only an astute businessman, he had style. When he was sure he was out of earshot, he took out his cell, prayed for a strong signal and dialed Kit. The moment his friend answered, Roman asked, "How soon can you get to Corfu?"

There were a couple of beats of silence. Then Kit said, "How soon do you need me there?"

That was why Kit was his best friend. "Yesterday." Then he filled him in on what was happening and what he needed him to do.

CASSANDRA ANGELIS HURRIED along the garden path until she reached the bench where she often sat to clarify her thoughts at the twilight hour. All day long she'd been thinking about Roman and Philly. And worrying. The danger that she'd twice seen swirling around them would reach its climax tonight. But shc'd had to put all thought of it out of her mind and deal with clients.

The huge house she'd inherited from her father sat on five acres of land atop a hill that offered a distant view of the Pacific. The garden had always been one of her favorite spots. Settling herself on the bench, she fixed her gaze on the blue water in the distance. The sky was streaked with shades of red and orange and the sun had just begun its descent into the sea.

Cass let her mind empty. Midnight, sunrise and sunset were when her visions were strongest. As the sun sank lower into the Pacific, the dimming light in front of her began to shift and swirl. This time it wasn't a sunlit beach that appeared, but a darker, colder place, filled with shadows. She could make out Philly. But the man who was grasping her arm wasn't Roman. He had his back to her so she couldn't see his face. But she sensed the stranger's emotions—greed, jealousy and a hunger for revenge that crossed over into the irrational. Laced through all of that, Cass sensed the purest evil she'd ever encountered.

Philly and the man weren't alone. She got a clear feeling about that just before the image faded. The shot that then rang out was so loud, so unexpected that Cass screamed.

"Cassandra?" Strong hands gripped her shoulders and gave her a gentle shake. Otherwise, Cass was almost sure she would have fainted.

Instead, she gathered her thoughts, opened her eyes and found herself looking at Mason Leone.

"Are you all right?" Mason asked.

Cass drew in a deep breath. "Yes. How long have you been here?"

He was still holding her shoulders, and she was grateful for the strength she felt in his hands. "Just a few minutes. You looked as though you were seeing something, so I didn't want to interrupt."

"I'm not sure what I saw. But they're in danger—Roman and Philly." Cass paused to suppress a shudder.

"I know," Mason said. "Kit sent me to tell you that he's joining them."

Cass blinked. "Kit sent you."

"He called and left messages for you, but he asked me to come over and make sure you knew. Roman arranged for him to fly to Corfu on a private plane that Oliver Enterprises occasionally charters. He left this morning."

"If something happens to them, I'll never forgive myself."

Mason frowned at her. "Why would you blame yourself? Just because you can see into the future doesn't mean that you've played a part in it."

"But I have. I've known for a long time that Roman and Philly were meant to be together, but I didn't just let the Fates handle it. I nudged both of them to go to Greece. I even enlisted Kit's help."

Mason studied her for a moment. Then he pulled her slowly into his arms. "Maybe that's what you were supposed to do. Maybe what you saw for them required a little intervention on your part."

"I suppose that's possible."

"Did you see anything definitive—one of them lying still or something like that?"

This time she couldn't suppress the shudder and Mason's arms tightened around her.

"No, thank heavens. But I heard a gunshot."

"Well, Kit took a gun with him. I gave it to him. I also supplied him with some stare-of-the-art surveillance equipment. Roman has a plan, and he and Roman know how to handle themselves."

Everything Mason said made sense, and Cass found that the tension and fear that she'd been feeling all day was draining out of her.

"Do you want me to join them?"

She raised her head then and met his eyes. "You'd do that?"

"Yes. But I don't think it's necessary."

Cass thought for a minute. "Neither do I."

"One other thing."

"Yes?"

"I'm a patient man, Cassandra. You can go on seeing Charlie Galvin until you make up your mind. I know what I want, and I can wait."

Then putting the lie to his words, Mason covered Cass's mouth with his.

13

IT WAS NEARLY MIDNIGHT before Roman and I were back on Gianni Stassis's yacht. Carlo Ferrante had taken off in his seaplane the moment we'd returned. Stassis had ordered a late supper and then explained that he wouldn't be joining us as he had to go back to Athens because of an early-morning business meeting. I sensed that was just an excuse to leave Roman and me alone. In addition to being a tycoon, Gianni was a kind and thoughtful man. Too bad his thoughtfulness was going to waste.

Ever since he'd agreed to my masquerading as the Princess Melina, Roman had distanced himself from me. I'd thoroughly enjoyed the shopping spree that Carlo and Gianni had taken me on. What woman wouldn't have? I'd felt just like Julia Roberts in *Pretty Woman,* choosing a whole new wardrobe in that exclusive store on Rodeo Drive. Only—even better—I was in Athens. I'd modeled each of the outfits for Carlo Ferrante and Gianni, but Roman had stood on the fringes and hadn't joined in the fun.

Now I was seated alone at the table Kyros had set up on the deck inside a three-sided tent for privacy. Candles flickered in glass hurricane lamps, champagne chilled in a silver bucket and lobster was arranged with several dipping sauces on a china platter. The sea was black and calm, and millions of stars studded the sky. On a nearby hill, an ancient temple was illuminated.

I was wearing a sleeveless white sheath that fit like a glove from just above my breasts to midthigh. Ferrante had declared it too casual for Magellan's party, but he'd signaled to the saleswoman to add it to his order, saying it would do for the plane trip back to Corfu in case Magellan had some of his men checking arrivals at the small airport. Before we'd left the boutique, Princess Melina Rinaldi's wardrobe had been completed with shoes, lingerie, and Carlo Ferrante had even loaned me a diamond necklace and matching earrings, insisting that I needed something expensive for the party at the Castello. He said he'd borrowed the jewelry from a friend before coming to Gianni's yacht, and I had to wonder if he'd been that confident we'd agree to his plan or if he was a man who was prepared for every eventuality.

I felt every inch the princess, and a Hollywood movie producer couldn't have ordered up a more romantic setting.

Yet Roman stood at the railing still talking on his cell phone. From eavesdropping on his side of the conversation, I deduced that he was filling Ionescu in on the masquerade we were planning. I was pretty sure he'd talked briefly to Kit and then for a longer length of time to his father.

But he wasn't talking to me. He'd made it clear that he wasn't happy with what we were going to do tomorrow, and I didn't know how to make that right. When he closed his cell, he didn't turn back to me. Instead, he leaned one arm on the railing and stared out at the calm sea.

He looked…different. In the tux Carlo had purchased for him, he looked elegant, but somehow more rugged—especially since he'd pulled the bow tie loose and opened the top three buttons of his shirt.

Roman hadn't commented on my transformation into

Princess Melina Rinaldi, and I hadn't commented on his into my bodyguard. But I liked it very much. The first time I'd gotten a good look at him in the salon, my mouth had watered. He'd looked tougher in a James Bond sort of way. I'd never thought of Roman as being dangerous before. I wondered if I looked different to him.

I experienced a sudden surge of impatience. Here I was dressed like a princess, and I had the perfect stage setting. Wasn't it time I acted as if I had royal blood? I rose and strode toward the railing. We were at another impasse of sorts, so either Melina or the new, improved Philly had to take an alternate approach. "You're upset with me."

The moon was behind him, throwing his face into shadow, but I could see the dark, angry gleam of his eyes when they met mine. "No. I'm upset that I agreed to this whole masquerade idea of Ferrante's. I don't trust him."

"Neither do I."

His eyes narrowed then. "You seemed to find him very charming."

I shrugged. "I wanted to go forward with the plan. So I let him think I was charmed. There's a hardness inside of him—except when it comes to animals. I wouldn't want to be one of his enemies. Did you buy what he told us about the jewels? Do you think they're really his and that he's waited all these years to use them to get his revenge on Magellan? The whole scenario he described about Magellan leaving him in the cave to die reminded me a bit of something right out of Edgar Allan Poe."

"'The Cask of Amontillado'?"

"Yes. Only, the victim gets to drown in a cave instead of being walled up in a catacomb. And if it's true, why didn't he go straight to the police?"

"I think the revenge part is true enough. What concerns

me most is what Ferrante didn't tell us. Animal lover or not, he's going to a lot of trouble to set up this masquerade just to let us rescue a cat."

"Have you forgotten that I'm supposed to bid on the jewels? That will get both Ionescu and Ferrante evidence of what Magellan really does at his parties."

"Perhaps. But Ionescu pointed out it will be the word of a fake princess against Andre Magellan. And I have a feeling that the picture Ferrante painted of how easily we can get Caliban out of the cave and escape is way too rosy."

I agreed, but I didn't say so. "I know there are elements of danger, but I don't see another way."

He sighed then. "Neither do I. And you're not going to be able to walk away from this as long as your cousins are in trouble, and Caliban is lying injured on that rock ledge. I understand that. So does Kit."

"Kit? You talked with him again? Did he have anything else on Magellan or Ferrante?"

"No. But I didn't just talk to your brother. I asked him to join us on Corfu tomorrow."

"He's coming to Greece? But then…" My heart sank. That could mean the abrupt end of Roman's and my idyllic affair. In effect, San Francisco was coming to us. What if Roman was reluctant to continue our relationship under the watchful eyes of my older brother? My temper bubbled up. I grabbed his shirtfront. "Why did you invite Kit here without telling me?"

He took my wrists and stilled my hands. Then he grinned at me. "Now you don't look like the cool Princess Melina. You look like my Philly."

His use of the word *my* slammed the brakes on my temper, but still I lifted my chin. "I didn't think you even noticed my transformation."

His eyes gleamed again, this time with heat instead of temper. "Oh, I noticed. The blond hair is very attractive."

My mouth went dry. "So is the thug look. You called me cool. Why do you say that?"

He released one of my hands to run his knuckles along my cheekbone. "With the blond hair and the blue contacts, you remind me of an ice princess." Then he dropped his hand. "Philly, about Kit—I had to call him. Gianni doesn't trust Ferrante, either. He advised me to have a backup plan. That's where your brother comes in. I haven't had body-guarding experience. He has. If Ferrante or Magellan tries something unexpected, Kit's our ace in the hole."

I understood what Roman was saying but the question that nearly popped out of my mouth was: *What about us?* At the last minute I pressed my lips together. That was a question the old Philly would have asked. And I wasn't that woman anymore. I knew what I wanted the answer to be. And I was going to find a way to make it happen.

In the meantime, tomorrow was a long time away.

I glanced over at the table that Kyros had so carefully set for us and an idea came to me. I met Roman's eyes. "You probably never played pretend games as a kid. The kind where you act out a story—like *Cinderella* or *Beauty and the Beast*?"

"As a matter of fact, Sadie used to nag me to play that kind of thing sometimes. After my mother died, my dad would occasionally put me in charge of both of my sisters on the nanny's day off. But I drew the line at acting out fairy tales. We used to play action-adventure movies. *Indiana Jones, Star Wars*—that kind of thing."

His answer surprised me. But I found I liked picturing Roman running around with his sisters. "Were you Luke Skywalker?"

"Only when I lost the coin toss. Sadie and I both wanted to be Han Solo."

"I knew there was a reason I like your sister. What roles did Juliana get?"

"Villains. She was the youngest." He released my hands and ran one finger along the line of my jaw. "Where are you going with this, Philly?"

"First of all, I'm not Philly. I'm Princess Melina Rinaldi, and you're my bodyguard, Marco. You call me Lee, and I'll call you Marc."

I reached up and pulled off his tie. "This is going to be a little different than acting out a fairy tale or a movie. I'm going to tell you the beginning—but we'll have to discover the ending together."

Actually, since I was making this up as I went along, I was going to have to discover the beginning also.

I held his gaze as I dropped the tie and drew his jacket off. "You've been working for me for six months now, and there's been this steadily growing attraction between us." I began to free the buttons of his shirt. "We don't talk about it, but it's there. Sometimes, I catch a hint of hunger in the way you look at me. And every time you touch me—even in the most casual of ways—a hand at the small of my back, an accidental brush of your finger on my skin, my insides go into a meltdown."

The fact that the story I was spinning was close to what had been happening between me and Roman for the past few days in reality had flames leaping to life inside of me.

"Your problem, Marc, is that you're too controlled. But I'm not. I like to reach out and take what I want." I ran my hands up his chest to his throat. Beneath my fingertips, his pulse pounded fiercely. I felt my own leap in response.

"So tonight, I've decided to make my move. I'm a bit

spoiled and used to getting my way. Part of the whole princess package. But I've chosen you as my new boy toy, and before we make love, I'm going to play with you. That's what toys are for, right?"

As I continued to talk, I began to feel my way into the role. Melina was a lot like me—impulsive—but she was spoiled, and bolder. The way she would make love to a man would be different.

"I've given the crew the night off, and I've commanded you to be here. You really have no choice if you want to keep your job." I slipped his shirt to the floor, and reached for his belt. "Now the pants. Do you know how many times I've undressed you in my imagination?"

"I'll bet not as many times as I've undressed you."

The rough edge to his voice had my fingers fumbling with his zipper.

"Just a minute." He slipped a hand into his pocket, pulled out condoms and offered them to me.

I took them and thinking quickly, stuffed them into the bodice of my dress. Then I met his eyes again. "Marc, you naughty boy. You must have anticipated why I invited you here tonight."

"I know that you want me." The heat in his eyes reminded me I was playing with fire.

"And I *so* wanted to surprise you. I'll have to think of something else."

Once the trousers had pooled at his feet, my throat went dry as dust. The black briefs were made of sheer silk and revealed clear evidence that he was ready for me. I was suddenly ready for him, too.

Not yet.

As he stepped out of the trousers, I focused on getting back into character.

"Lee."

The thrill that shot through me when he used the name was enough to curl my toes. But when he gripped my upper arms to draw me closer, it was my turn to still *his* hands. I smiled up at him. "I forgot to mention one little thing. You can't touch me or kiss me until I give you permission. But I can touch you." And I did. I trailed my hands down to his waist, danced them along the waistband of his briefs and kissed his throat just where the pulse was beating.

"I've waited so long to do this." I wasn't sure if it was Philly or Lee speaking. When I inhaled his scent—so strong, so male—I nearly lost my train of thought for the second time. Before I did, I closed my fingers around his wrist, then turned and walked toward the table. "Let's have some champagne, shall we?" I didn't want this to end too soon—at least not until I figured out what Melina would do next.

I urged him beneath the canopy and onto the cushioned bench that ran along the side of the boat. We were screened from the shore, facing a wide expanse of sea. The candles were half burned down so I blew them out before I knelt beside…Marc. While I filled a glass with the champagne, I rested my hand on his thigh, then let it slide until I felt the hard length of his erection beneath my palm. Oh, yes, Lee was much bolder than I usually was.

When I felt him grow even harder, heat pooled in my center, and overflowed, along with the glass. I lifted it to offer him a drink, and some spilled on his shoulder.

He took a sip of the champagne, and so did I. After placing the glass back on the table, I hiked up the skirt of my dress around my waist and straddled his thighs. His entire body bucked as he became aware I wasn't wearing panties. Angling my hips I felt his penis press against my center. Immediately, I wanted more. And I could have more.

All I had to do was give my permission. But not yet. How far could I push him before he decided to break the rules I'd made?

Rubbing against him, I leaned down to lick a drip of champagne off of his chin. The flavor was darker, more potent than it had been from the glass.

Curious, I closed my mouth over what I'd spilled on his shoulder. There was a different flavor there, warmer, richer. His erection jerked and grew harder, reminding me that I wanted to taste that, too.

Lifting my head, I met his eyes. "You make the champagne taste so much better."

"How much longer are you going to play with me?"

"Just a little longer." I was amazed I'd gotten this far.

With a sudden movement of his hips, he pushed his penis just inside my entrance. I felt as if I were suddenly trapped in a furnace. The only barrier between us was the thin silk of his briefs. For a moment neither one of us moved. I even forgot to breathe. The temptation to lift my hips, shove down his briefs and lower myself onto him was huge.

But so was the temptation to play just a little while longer. I snagged the glass of champagne, wiggled off his lap onto the deck and found a position for myself between his legs.

ROMAN KNEW what she was going to do next even before she began to lower his briefs. Anticipation of the pleasure weakened him as her nails scraped his skin. Initially, the erotic story of the spoiled princess and her boy toy hadn't intrigued him. But it hadn't taken her long to stoke his desire to the flash point.

Perhaps it was the contrast between the ice-princess facade and the boldness of her touch. The memory of her wet heat rubbing against him had heightened every sensation—the scrape of her nails as she pulled down his briefs, the warmth of her breath on the tip of his penis. How could the woman kneeling between his legs right now be the same imp who'd stripped for him on the plane? And how could she make him want this much? Until his whole body ached and throbbed and threatened to shatter?

He dug his fingers into the cushioned seat as she finally grasped him in her hands. The splash of icy champagne had him arching up. Then his vision grayed as he watched her take him into his mouth. Sensations battered him—the softness of her lips, the murmurs of pleasure she made as she laved him with her tongue. And there was such heat. It exploded through him like a rush of lava, and he was sure he felt himself melting, sinew, blood and bone. In another moment…

I WAS UNDER HIM on the deck floor with such speed that I couldn't recall the motion—only the hard press of his body on mine.

"Rules suspended," he gasped as he dragged the condom out of my dress and tore it open with his teeth.

"Hurry," I said. The movement of his fingers against me as he sheathed himself had me arching, aching. "I need you…"

He plunged into me and tossed me into a world of sharp sensations. I felt everything—the planks of the deck beneath me, his ragged breath at my ear, those long fingers pressing into my hips. And most of all I felt Roman inside of me, thrusting again and again. That was all I wanted, everything I wanted.

"Come with me, Philly. I need you with me."

Caught in the world of pleasure he'd taken me to, I whispered, "Always." And then I shattered.

14

SHE SLEPT like an infant—hard and deep. Roman sipped his coffee and watched her. She was stretched full length on the sofa across from his, her hand tucked beneath her cheek as Gianni's plane carried them back to Corfu. For the trip, she'd changed back into her own clothes, slacks and a T-shirt. But the hair was still exotically Princess Melinda Rinaldi's.

It occurred to Roman that it was the first time he'd ever watched her sleep. They'd never given each other any time for that. The features of her face were so delicate, her body so slender. For once, she looked fragile to him.

Perhaps it was the blond hair, he mused. Philly always projected such energy, such enthusiasm, and a strength and courage that continued to amaze him.

Then there was the passion and emotion that simmered below the surface. He'd always been aware of it, of course. Passion ran deep in the Angelis family. But in the seven years he'd known her, none of the guilty fantasies he'd spun about making love to Philly had approached the reality. Each time they came together, she surprised him. Fascinated him. The erotic fantasy she'd woven for them last night was still playing at the edges his mind.

Later, he'd carried her downstairs to one of the bedrooms and held her close until sleep claimed them both.

A little before dawn, she'd nudged him awake and climbed on top of him.

"One more time," she'd whispered in his ear. And then she'd made love to him as if she was sure it would be the last time. She'd teased him using her mouth on his flesh until he was shivering, aching. As she'd moved down his body, murmuring her pleasure, she'd drawn more from him than desire. She'd pulled all his emotions to the surface. His throat had stung with them.

When she'd finally taken him inside of her, it was his heart that had melted. He hadn't been able to take his eyes off of her. In the moonlight, with her white skin and bright eyes, she might have been a powerful goddess—Athena, Aphrodite. She could have asked anything of him, and he would have given it. When she'd arched back, taking more of him in, he was hers.

He'd watched her shudder with pleasure. Then they'd begun to move—not in a race, but in a slow journey. With one mind, they strove to hang on to each moment, each new thrill, and when they'd finally reached the summit, they'd tumbled over together.

Roman heard the change in the sound of the plane's engines and felt the shift in the cabin that signaled their descent. Still, he continued to study her. In and out of bed, he was beginning to know Philly as a woman of many facets. Just in the short time they'd been in Greece, he'd found her to be strong and incredibly brave. Braver than he was, perhaps. She certainly didn't seem to have any qualms about the masquerade they were going to act out tonight.

He'd taken every precaution he could think of, but he was still uneasy. One thing he and Kit had agreed on—at the least sign of trouble, their first priority would be to get her out of there.

When the jet hit a little bump, she stirred, then sat up. He watched the cloudy blue eyes clear and then focus. "How much longer?"

"We've started our descent. Kit and Ionescu will meet us at the plane."

Disappointment, then resignation flooded her eyes. "Big brother."

"Our backup," he reminded her.

"Is he going to introduce himself to Miranda as Roman Oliver, or will he turn us in right away?"

"We're not going to the Villa Prospero until after the party," he explained. "Our pilot has already reported a mechanical problem to the airfield. The inspector and Kit will come aboard as mechanics. We'll dress and leave for the party from here. Kit will replace Gianni's man as our driver."

Her brows shot up. "You're being very thorough."

He leaned forward then. "Yes. This isn't a game of Let's Pretend." He reached over and took her hand, needing the contact. "Ionescu has his agenda and so do Ferrante and Magellan. Kit's and my agenda is solely to keep you safe."

"Not one but two big brothers."

Something in her tone made him want to frown. And he thought then of the deal she'd made with him—that their relationship would only last while they were in Greece. Then, as she'd put it during that fateful dinner, they'd go back to "big brother, little sister" and she'd walk away.

Not bloody likely, Roman thought. But this wasn't the time or the place to talk about it. He promised himself they'd have that discussion as soon as they were safely out of the Castello Corli tonight.

The plane bumped down on the runway.

NERVES ALWAYS made me hungry. I located ham, cheese and rye bread in the galley and lined them up on the counter. Truth be told, I was a bit bored. For the last hour, my brother Kit, Inspector Ionescu and Roman had been playing with the surveillance "toys" that Kit had brought. He and the inspector had boarded the plane wearing work overalls and caps and carrying toolboxes.

I glanced over to see that the men were still huddled over the electronic equipment. To my way of thinking a microphone was a microphone. The fact that it was tiny enough that I could tape it between my breasts was convenient, but not particularly fascinating. I was going to be "wired" the whole time I was at Andre Magellan's party. Everything he said to me would be recorded.

After several minutes, I'd excused Ariel and myself to check on my wardrobe for the party and then she'd fallen asleep on the pillows in the bedroom.

Poor thing. Standing vigil over Caliban for the last three days had taken its toll on her. Ionescu had smuggled Ariel onto the plane in his toolbox, and she hadn't been happy with him. But she'd calmed down when I'd assured her that we were going to get Caliban out of that cave tonight. Roman and I were going to take her with us. He didn't want to take any chances that she wouldn't be around to guide us when we got to the Castello.

Having Ionescu bring Ariel to the plane was just one more example of just how thorough Roman was being. Because he was worried. The fact that I wanted badly to soothe his nerves was only making my own jumpier.

It was nearly seven—another two hours before we'd leave for the Castello. We were going to arrive fashionably late. Then we could rescue Caliban under cover of darkness. That was the plan, and I was anxious to put it into action.

A glance into the main cabin assured me that the men's fascination with the electronic equipment hadn't faded. They still had their heads together around one of the tables. Inspector Ionescu managed to look dapper even in work clothes. And my brother Kit—well, he managed to look incredibly handsome in anything he wore. Of my three brothers, he was the one I was closest to. And in spite of the fact that I'd originally had mixed feelings about his arrival, I was glad that he was here.

Turning back to my sandwich making, I found mustard in the small galley refrigerator and slathered it on one slice of rye bread. Then I piled meat and cheese on the other. I had just sliced my masterpiece in half when Kit joined me and snagged the bigger section.

"Thanks, sis."

"You could make your own."

He grinned at me. "Yeah. But yours always taste better. Anyway, you're just eating because you're nervous."

"Know-it-all," I muttered. But that was the thing about my big brothers. They knew me very well.

"By the way, I like the blond look."

"Thanks," I said around a mouthful.

He settled his hip against the counter and stretched out his long legs until the base of the other counter blocked him. "Close quarters."

My gaze dropped to the floor and I remembered just how "close" the space had been when Roman and I had made love on our flight to Athens.

I felt the heat flood my cheeks so I turned away to open a bottle of water for each of us.

"There's really no need to be nervous," he said.

"I know."

"We're going to have your back. Ionescu will have a couple of men stationed on the other side of the wall just a ways down from the gate. Once we have Caliban, Roman and I will rig something to get him over the wall. When that part of our mission is accomplished, we'll go on to part two."

I drank some of my water. "The inspector's very cooperative and eager to help all of a sudden. Yesterday, he wouldn't even go up and ask if we could search the grounds."

"He wants evidence that will prove that Magellan is fencing the jewels from these high-profile robberies. Roman has convinced him that with the wire you're wearing he has a good chance of getting it. Once you get the evidence he needs, Ionescu will send his men in."

Having her wear a microphone had been Roman's idea, too. Kit had merely provided the state-of-the-art equipment.

"Roman is worried. I wish I could do something about that." I glanced over at the table where Ionescu and Roman were studying what looked to be some kind of map. "What is that?"

"It's a drawing of the grounds and the first floor of the Castello."

"He's being so thorough."

"That's the way Roman always is. He's said to me many times that knowledge is power. He wouldn't walk into a business meeting unprepared—he's definitely not going to step foot on the grounds of the Castello Corli without knowing everything he can. Ionescu and I are just the backup in this little operation. Roman's in charge. If he weren't, I wouldn't agree to letting my sister run the kind of risk you're going to run tonight."

Something warm and sweet moved through me. "He's amazing."

"I've always thought so." Kit cleared his throat. "How are things going between the two of you?"

I shifted my gaze to his. "What do you mean?"

"Philly, when I went to Ionescu's office, I had to introduce myself to my cousin Alexi as Roman Oliver. I know all about the lie Roman told Miranda so that he could share your room. I'm assuming that you took advantage of what the Fates offered."

My eyes widened.

"In fact, I'm hoping you did."

I think my mouth dropped open. "How did you…"

He grinned at me again. "I'm a trained investigator, remember? For starters, there is so much sexual energy whenever the two of you are in the same room, it's a wonder that something doesn't ignite. Then there was the fact that when I told Roman that you were off to Greece to find your true love just as our mother and Aunt Cass had, he was on the next flight here."

"Because he felt he had to protect me—like a brother would."

Kit's grin widened. "Except that none of your real brothers hightailed it to Corfu. You should have seen his face. He turned white as a sheet when I told him about your plan. And it was the first time since I've known him that he was at a total loss for words."

I returned my gaze to Roman, and I began to see everything that had happened between us from a slightly different perspective.

THE MAIN HOUSE of the Castello Corli was lit up like the palace in a fairy tale as we drove through the gates. Kit was behind the wheel of Gianni Stassis's car, Roman sat beside me in his tuxedo, and Ariel was tucked beneath the long black cloak I was wearing.

As soon as we were out of sight of the guards, Kit pulled the car as far off the road as he could. Fortunately for us, the driveway to the Castello was circular and lined on either side with trees. Kit had been instructed by Magellan's men to proceed to the front entrance to drop us off and then follow the directions of the guards there for parking. Roman's plan was to delay our arrival until we'd rescued Caliban. We all exited the car.

The Fates were smiling on us in one sense because storm clouds had blanketed the sky. Darkness and the breeze rustling the cypress leaves masked our movements. But the threat of rain meant we had to work quickly or get caught in a sudden downpour. Using the trees for cover, Kit led us toward the tower where Ferrante had said there was a second entrance to the cave.

Getting past the guard shack was tricky. A limo stopped halfway through the gate was shining its headlights right across our path. Kit held up a hand and we waited until it passed us and moved up the driveway. Then we took our chance and dashed for the trees on the other side of the entrance.

I released Ariel and she took the lead.

We moved as quickly as we could, but each second seemed like an eternity. I stumbled once and Roman gripped my arm to steady me. When we were deep enough into the trees, Kit took out a pencil-size flashlight and played it back and forth in front of us. Overhead, the wind was picking up, and I'd lost sight of Ariel.

This way.

"She's still ahead of us," I said, searching the darkness for a flash of white.

Suddenly, the trees thinned, and there she was. The tower was about twenty yards ahead of us, and the walls of the old fortress abutted it on two sides. As we approached, Kit's flashlight illuminated a section at the tower's base that had crumbled. My heart took a hopeful leap when I caught a glimpse of the stone stairs descending into the darkness.

I squatted to be closer to Ariel. *Show us where he is.*

She disappeared into the opening.

Kit put the flashlight between his teeth. Roman couldn't risk messing up his tux, so Kit was going to go after Caliban. First we lost sight of him and then of all trace of the light.

"You okay?" Roman spoke softly into the microphone he was wearing.

"Yeah." I wasn't wearing a receiver, but I could just hear Kit's voice. "I've run out of stairs. Wait. There's a rope ladder."

Squatting again, I spoke into the opening. "Do you see any sign of Ariel or Caliban or the rock ledge?" I asked. I could picture all three in my mind.

Kit said nothing further for the space of five endless beats. Then we heard a grunt. I stopped breathing.

"Easy, fella." In the same soft tone, he said, "Philly, see if you can settle him. He doesn't look happy to see me."

I calmed my mind, pushing everything else out. *Ariel, tell him we're here to help.*

A moment later, Kit said, "Got him." Then he added, "Shit! I lost the flashlight."

I didn't let out the breath I was holding until Kit's head reappeared in the crumbled opening at the foot of the tower. My hands trembled as I held them out for Caliban. I could feel Ariel's anxiety. My own nearly matched it.

I checked the pulse at Caliban's throat. It was strong and steady. His eyes were open and on mine. *I'm Philly.*

For the first time, I felt a clear connection with him. Though he communicated nothing in words, I could tell the pain was centered in his leg, just as I'd envisioned. "His leg is injured, and he's cold." But overall, he seemed a lot calmer about his ordeal than Ariel was. If Ariel reminded me of my cat Pretzels, Caliban was more like Peanuts.

You're going to be fine.

His eyes gleamed at me. Then he let out a long breath and closed them.

Roman took my arm. "This way."

We felt our way along the wall until we could make out the lights of the guard shack through the trees. One of Ionescu's men was supposed to be posted on the other side about fifty yards from the Castello's entrance. Working quickly, we fashioned a sling of sorts out of my cloak, placed Caliban in it, and Kit slipped it on. Then Roman boosted my brother onto his shoulders, and Kit managed to muscle his way to the top of the fortress wall. The sky above was so black that I could only locate Kit's position when Ariel leaped from the branch of a tree to join him.

Seconds ticked by before I heard a noise I recognized as my brother's imitation of a birdcall. The only response was the rustle of cypress leaves overhead.

Then I thought I caught the faint sound of a man's voice and some kind of movement on the top of the wall. The wind had picked up, and I could hear the rumble of thunder in the distance. Finally, Kit dropped lightly to the ground beside us. "Mission accomplished. Within minutes, Caliban will be on his way to a vet in Myrtos."

The relief that streamed through me nearly had my knees buckling. Roman gripped my arm, urging me deeper into the trees.

Wait.

The word came through very clearly and I whirled back. It was only because of Ariel's white fur that I saw she was still on the top of the wall. She leaped to the branch of a tree and then to the Castello grounds.

"Ariel's going to hang around," I explained to Roman and Kit.

Roman glanced back at the wall. "Tell her to stay out of sight."

I relayed the message to Ariel as Roman pulled me into the trees.

GLITTER. GLAMOUR. They were everywhere one looked in the ballroom of the Castello Corli. And Roman had spent the last thirty minutes looking very carefully. To his way of thinking, there were too many exits. The storm that had been threatening earlier had passed on, and the French doors that lined the room on either side had been thrown open to the terraces.

Inside the ballroom, light glimmered from crystal chandeliers and flickered from thick white candles. Masses of flowers surrounded the columns that edged a marble floor the length of a football field, and their scents mixed with exotic perfumes and the more savory aromas on the trays a small army of servants carried throughout the room.

Whatever one might say or suspect about Andre Magellan, the man knew how to throw a hell of a party. And how to cut a dramatic figure. He wore his long hair loose and it fell to his shoulders. His open-throated red silk shirt made a perfect frame for a diamond the size of a robin's egg. And the contrast of the shirt against his white tuxedo made him easy to locate and track in the crowd. Since each guest descended a marble stairway, Andre Magellan also had ample time to study new arrivals before they disappeared into the crowd that now filled the ballroom.

He'd been standing at the far end of the ballroom when Philly had descended the stairs, and for just an instant, Roman thought he'd seen surprise on Magellan's face. That worried him a bit. Ferrante had assured them that Princess Melina Rinaldi was an invited and expected guest.

So far Magellan had kept his distance, playing the good host by smiling at some guests and lingering longer with others. If he was accepting silent bids on a priceless cache of jewels, there was no outward sign of it.

But if Ferrante had been telling the truth, Magellan had had several years to polish his act. And there were many possible buyers among the guests who ran the gamut from politicians and rulers of small countries to several celebrities with a star on the Hollywood Walk of Fame. One of them, an actor Roman recalled from a series of successful action-adventure movies, had been talking to Philly for the last five minutes. When he raised her hand to his lips and kissed her fingers, Roman moved closer.

"I've so enjoyed meeting you," Philly said. "But I really have to say hello to my host."

"Till we meet again," the young star said before moving away.

"Nicely done," Roman murmured.

"Thanks, Marc."

"Magellan is allowing you to come to him."

"Yeah, I got that. But there's nothing that says I have to rush." She snagged a glass of wine from the tray of a passing servant.

"You're really getting into this, aren't you?"

"I'm enjoying being a princess."

It occurred to Roman that princess was only one of the many roles she'd decided to play since he'd joined her in Greece. And she played each one so well. Right now, she was giving every indication of having the time of her life. He wondered how much of it was playacting and how much was just how Philly Angelis met every new experience that came her way. There were so many facets to her that he'd never seen before—or never allowed himself to see. Once they left Greece, would he get the opportunity to discover any more?

He knew her well enough now to understand that rescuing Caliban and getting Alexi out of jail had been her main objectives. She wasn't nearly as worried about trapping Magellan into saying something incriminating. But that was the part Roman was worried about.

Since he wasn't the Princess Melina Rinaldi's escort but Marco, her chief of security, he kept a discreet distance of about two feet behind her right shoulder as she wove her way through the crowd. As they progressed, the backless, sequined dress captured more than one male eye, and several men stopped her to talk.

In the end it was Magellan who came to them. Roman noted that the hand that had trembled earlier when she'd taken Caliban from Kit held steady when she offered it to their host. Roman knew that she had the bid for the jewels with the amount that Ferrante had written in the palm of her hand. Andre had it in his by the time he kissed her fingers. She was handling everything like a pro.

The smile Magellan beamed at her held a practiced charm. "Princess Rinaldi, my apologies for taking so long to welcome you to my home."

Philly smiled right back. "Call me Melina, please. And no apology needed."

"You are most gracious." He took the glass of wine from her hand and passed it to Roman. Then he led Philly out onto the dance floor and swept her into the throng of dancers.

"He's made his move. They're dancing." Edging his way around other couples on the floor, Roman spoke into the microphone attached to his tie. "Where are you?"

"I'm just outside on the terrace, south side of the building. Want me to slip in?" Kit asked.

"No. Just hold your position."

Then it was Magellan's voice Roman heard in his ear. "I expected you to have an Italian accent."

"My mother was English, so I grew up bilingual."

"And you're much more beautiful than your photos."

"Then I'll have to fire the photographer."

Magellan laughed. "You're not only beautiful but refreshing."

He was grilling her, Roman thought. Ferrante had assured them that his cousin was camera shy. Where had Magellan gotten hold of photos? Had Ferrante lied or merely slipped up? Roman started to elbow his way more forcefully along the edge of the dance floor as Magellan moved Philly farther and farther away from him.

"Why is it that we've never run into one another before?" Magellan asked.

"I'm really a homebody. I only travel when something interests me. Jewelry always interests me."

"Ah, yes," Magellan said. "The diamonds you're wearing are truly breathtaking. I keep thinking that I've seen them before."

"I hardly think so. Since I don't attend many parties, they spend most of their time in a safe."

Roman saw him run one finger along the length of the diamond choker Ferrante had insisted she wear. "That seems such a waste. They were made to see the light of day—or evening."

"I agree. That's why I wore them tonight."

She was holding her own, Roman thought.

"How good is my bid?" she asked.

And she was doing her job.

"It's very good."

Roman was still the width of the dance floor away when Magellan swept her out through the French doors onto the terrace. Roman pushed couples out of his way as he crossed the floor. "She's out of my sight," he said softly to Kit. "He's got her on the north terrace."

"I'm on it," Kit muttered.

Precious minutes ticked by as Roman zigged and zagged his way to the opened doors. By the time he made it onto the terrace, both Magellan and Philly had disappeared.

15

Once we reached the terrace, Andre Magellan took my arm and guided me to the left. I had to double step to keep up with him. "Where are we going?" I asked.

"Just to my office. I want to discuss your bid."

"Excellent." That was Melina talking. As Philly, I wasn't sure I liked the sound of that. I'd seen him deftly unfold the piece of paper and glance at it while we were dancing. But a private chat about it certainly hadn't been part of the scenario that Carlo Ferrante had sketched out.

I was wired, I reminded myself. Roman could hear everything Magellan or I said. Any minute he was going to step out of the ballroom and insist on accompanying me. An armed guard stood at the far end of the terrace. Andre passed right by him, stepped behind a potted tree and inserted a key into a small iron door. As he pushed it open, I took the opportunity to glance back. There was no sign of Roman or Kit. Nerves began to bubble in my stomach when I realized that the door wouldn't be immediately visible to either of them. In fact, it was very well camouflaged. Purposefully?

Andre touched a switch and ushered me into a large windowless room lined with bookshelves. A huge, carved wooden desk looked as if it might have been among the original furnishings of the castle. The chair behind it resembled a throne. Light poured down from a large crystal chandelier. A quick glance around told me the only door was the one we'd entered through.

Persian rugs covered the stone floor, and there was a conference table that would have done King Arthur proud. The leather couches and chairs scattered throughout the room were more modern and looked to be quite comfortable. In spite of all the elegance, the room could easily serve as a prison. Someone locked in here would be at the mercy of her captor.

When I felt panic bubbling up, I slammed the brakes on the direction my thoughts were taking. Those were the old Philly's thoughts, and I was Princess Melina Rinaldi. I'd just handed Andre Magellan a bid on a priceless collection of jewels, and he'd brought me here to conduct business. I should be excited about that.

Plus, I had a job to do, I reminded myself. Up until Kit had jumped down from the Castello wall and assured me that Caliban was on his way to a vet, I'd been focused on rescuing Ariel's brother. I hadn't spent much time thinking about what Kit had referred to as "part two" of our mission tonight.

If I could get Andre Magellan to incriminate himself, Alexi would go free and I would have had a hand in punishing the man who'd hurt Caliban, and killed Ferrante's investigator Antony Delos.

Talk. You have to let Roman and Kit know where you are.

"This is a lovely room," I said. "And so surprising. Who would have expected it to be tucked away behind that potted tree. And the door—it was so small. It reminded me of the entrance to *The Secret Garden*. Do you remember reading that book as a child?"

"No." For the first time, I heard an undercurrent of anger in his voice as Andre walked behind the desk, opened a drawer and took out a file. He tossed it down on the desk, then turned and pressed something that had a wooden panel moving aside. Behind it was a fully stocked bar. "Would you like a drink?"

Melina would, I was sure. "Do you have white wine?"

"A very nice Italian one as a matter of fact. As I recall, you used to prefer Italian whites."

I used to prefer Italian whites? "What are you talking about? We've never met before."

He poured two glasses with practiced skill, then circled the desk to join me on the other side. He handed me one and raised his in a toast. "To games."

I let a puzzled frown appear on my forehead. "To games? I thought we came here to discuss my bid."

The smile he sent me didn't reach his eyes. "There's no need to discuss it. Yours is the highest. I knew the moment I saw you that it would be. Carlo would see to that."

ROMAN SWORE under his breath. The highest bid? Carlo Ferrante hadn't mentioned that little detail. Melina was just supposed to offer a bid and gather evidence. And it couldn't be an accident. Of all people, Ferrante would know what figure would top all the others in an auction of his own jewels.

Whatever the game was that the two men were playing, he knew that he had to get Philly away from Magellan as soon as possible. The doors through which they had exited had been in the center of the ballroom, so he had no idea in which direction they'd gone. There were armed guards stationed at either end of the terrace. After mentally flipping a coin, Roman headed to his right. He reached the guard just in time to see Kit approach from behind and knock the man out with the butt of his gun.

Together they dragged the body behind a potted palm. "And here I thought the P.I. business mostly involved tailing cheating spouses," Roman said. "I had no idea how talented you were."

"Necessity is the mother of invention. That's the first time I've ever had to do something like that."

"Philly said they went through a small iron door hidden behind a potted tree."

"Iron? Let's hope it's unlocked," Kit murmured. They searched behind several more trees, but found no door.

"AND JUST HOW did you know that my bid would be the highest without even seeing it?"

"Because Carlo sent you."

My stomach did a little flip, but I managed to keep my expression puzzled. "Carlo who?"

Andre set his glass on the desk so forcefully that the stem broke and wine spread over the surface. Ignoring it, he pushed the file closer to me. Then he flipped it open and pointed to a photograph. "This is Princess Melina Rinaldi."

The woman in the picture was a tall brunette who was at least ten years older and forty pounds heavier than I was. Okay. Not so good. I wished I could figure out who was lying—Carlo or Andre? All of the above?

I met Andre's eyes. "I'm Princess Melina Rinaldi. And since I've just placed the winning bid, I'd like to see the jewels."

"All in good time." He moved closer and once more ran a finger along my diamond choker.

I had to concentrate hard to suppress a shudder.

"You're nearly perfect." He circled the desk and took a framed picture off one of the shelves. "This is why I brought you here—so that you could see this."

Lie with Me

When he handed it to me, I simply stared down at it.

"We had it taken shortly after we arrived at Oxford."

I was seeing Andre and Carlo as they'd appeared fifteen years ago. And standing between them, laughing at the camera—was a blond-haired, blue-eyed young woman who looked just like me.

"She's Isabella Carlini," Andre said. "And she was my lover until Carlo seduced her."

Oh my, I thought, and racked my brains for something to say. But I didn't need to say anything. Magellan was doing all the talking—to himself more than to me.

"He blamed me for killing his damn horse, so he destroyed the only woman I've ever loved. He killed her." He ran his hands through his hair. "And he sent *you* here tonight to rattle me. To prove that he can still play the game better than I can."

It looked to me as if Carlo's rattling plan was working. Andre had begun to pace, and his temper was bubbling very close to the surface. He moved to the bar, poured himself a fresh glass of wine and drained it.

"Carlo always plays the game so very well. I try very hard to anticipate his moves. I knew the moment that the real Princess Rinaldi contacted me that Carlo had arranged it. They're related, after all. But when you walked in…I didn't expect it."

Which was just what Carlo had wanted. My mind was racing. He must have seen the resemblance between Isabella and me when he visited my Web site. That was why he'd agreed to meet with Roman and me. And then he'd turned me into her.

Magellan stopped pacing and moved toward me again. "The diamonds are a nice touch. I gave them to Isabella. I was going to marry her, you see. They were never recovered after Carlo murdered her."

"He murdered her?"

"Oh, yes. He told me all about it. Bragged about it. After he had to put down that stupid horse of his, he wanted revenge. So first he seduced Isabella. More than that, he made her fall in love with him. Then when he was sure I knew about it, he invited her to his room and told her she'd served her purpose. He was through with her. What he didn't mention was that he'd sabotaged the brakes on her car, so when she ran out of his room and drove away, she had no idea her car was going to end up wrapped around a tree."

For a moment, I couldn't think of anything to say. I could see that Andre was back in the past, reliving a painful memory. But I had to say something. Just because I was unmasked and in the middle of some kind of game that Carlo and Andre were playing didn't mean that I could forget my job.

"So that's why you stole Carlo's family jewels? To exact revenge for Isabella's death?"

He came back to the present then. "Partly. I also stole them to make money. I had a bid that night that was almost as high as yours."

"So Carlo was right. You do use these parties to fence stolen property."

Andre shrugged. "It's a very profitable business and much more exciting than banking. Five years ago, I could have made a fortune on Carlo's family jewels, and he would have had to live with the knowledge that someone else possessed something that belonged to him. Just as I had to live with the knowledge that he had possessed Isabella who'd belonged to me. But in the end I decided to let Carlo have them back so that I could show him that I could steal them again. He's been waiting ever since for me to make my move. Revenge is better when it occurs slowly, over time."

The rage in his eyes was so cold that I badly wanted to make a run for the door. Where was Roman? "Carlo said you left him in the cave to die."

Andre's eyes narrowed. "He seems to have confided a lot in you."

"Is it true? Did you try to kill him?"

"No. I didn't hit him that hard. I knew he had a better-than-even chance of escaping. It's all about the game, you see. Someday, I will have to kill him, I suppose. But then I won't have anyone to play with."

The calm way he spoke chilled me to the bone. Kit had been right. Andre and Carlo were two peas in a pod. And they were both top-of-the-line loony tunes.

"I gave him better odds that night than he gave Isabella." He touched my necklace again. "To think that he's had them all this time. And he had the nerve to send you to me wearing them." His voice was controlled, but the cold rage in his eyes was so near the surface that I took a step back.

He ran his hand through his hair, then pressed fingers against his temples. "I can't let anger blind me. I can't let him win again. Not this time."

Drawing in a deep breath, he moved behind his desk and opened a drawer. The gun he pulled out was small but deadly looking. *Think. Think.* A dash to the door was out at this point. I stood watching in frozen silence as he tucked the weapon into his pocket.

Andre circled the desk and grabbed my arm. "Come, we'll finish this part of the game. I'll take you to see the jewels."

"SHE'S GOT HIM," Roman murmured to Kit. "He just told her that he's going to take her to see the jewels. Ionescu will be able to arrest him."

Roman kept his gaze fixed on the potted trees ahead of them. At any moment Magellan and Philly should be stepping out of the room he'd taken her to. "You take Magellan," he murmured to Kit. "I'll get Philly." There was no way he was going to let her climb down into that cave with a crazy man. Ionescu and his men could rescue the damn jewels.

But as the seconds ticked by, neither Magellan nor Philly appeared on the terrace. The fear that had settled into his system the moment Magellan had waltzed her onto the terrace kept growing. Then he spotted Ariel sitting to the right of the first potted tree. An armed guard stood to the left.

"Want to bet that's it?" Kit asked in an undertone.

"Yeah." Roman hoped to hell that it was.

"You got a plan?" Kit asked under his breath as they neared the guard.

"Follow my lead." Roman didn't stop until he was right in front of the armed man. Then without warning, he whirled and threw a punch to the guy's jaw, quickly followed with a jab to his belly. When the surprised guard doubled over in pain, Roman brought his knee up to the guy's chin and the man fell like a rock.

"I'm impressed," Kit said.

"Me, too." Roman located the small door behind the potted tree. He turned the handle and found it locked.

In his ear, he heard Philly's voice again. "Where are we going? What is this? A secret passage? Does this lead to the smugglers' cave?"

"Indeed. And Carlo knows nothing about it. But I'm sure he's waiting for us there. He will have accessed it by the rope ladder or made his way in by the sea. But he'll be there just as he was the last time. So we'll go to him. After you, my dear Isabella."

Roman threw all his weight against the door. Then Kit gave it a try.

"It's no use," Roman said. "He's taking her through a secret passage to the smugglers' cave. We'll have to use the tower entrance. Magellan believes that Carlo will be waiting for them."

Together, they raced off the terrace and across the grounds. A couple of guards called out to them, but they paid them no heed. Roman was banking on the fact that the guards would stop short of gunning down guests during a party.

When they reached the tower, Ariel was already standing at the entrance.

Roman quickly turned to Kit. "You go signal Ionescu's men. Tell them that Philly's got Magellan recorded admitting to fencing jewels and he's taking her to the cave. We need backup."

"Will do." Kit was already moving. "Then I'll come back."

As soon as he'd disappeared into the trees, Roman squatted in front of Ariel. Philly always said that first she calmed her mind, so he tried to do the same. Hell, he wasn't a pet psychic, but maybe the cat would understand anyway.

"The bad man who hit Caliban with the gun has Philly. She's in trouble and he's taking her to the cave."

Ariel turned and disappeared into the opening.

Roman followed, pressing his hands to the granite walls as he made his way down stone steps. It was pitch-black inside. He remembered that Kit said the stairs ended abruptly, so he made his way slowly, feeling for each slab of stone. Sure enough, after ten steps, his foot felt nothing but air. Still keeping one hand braced against a wall, he squatted and located the rope ladder.

It was then that he heard the cat. Not in his head the way Philly would have. Ariel seemed to be aware of his communication handicap and so she was meowing softly. He assumed she was on a nearby rock ledge.

As he descended farther and farther into the darkness, Ariel always seemed to be nearby, making known her presence with soft, deep-throated purrs. It was slow going, mostly because he couldn't see a thing. Each time he lowered his foot he had to waste precious minutes feeling for a secure toehold on the next rung.

Urgency churned inside of him. He couldn't shake off the fear that Philly was in mortal danger. It wasn't so much anything Magellan had said to her. He hadn't made any overt threat. But Philly's resemblance to Isabella had obviously stirred memories in Andre Magellan. There'd been something in his tone when he'd been speaking of his former lover that had Roman wanting to hurry.

His right shoe slid off the rope, and for three breathless beats, he hung dangling in space before he found another rung.

Ariel purred softly.

"I'm okay." For the next few minutes, he focused his mind totally on the job. Gradually, he got a sense that the cave was widening. When he reached out with his hand, he could only feel the wall to his right. He took that as a sign of progress. He also thought that the space below him was growing lighter. But that could have been wishful thinking. The strongest feeling he had was that Ariel was growing impatient with him.

"I have to go slowly here," he explained to her in a soft voice. "If I make a misstep, I won't be of any use to Philly."

"Meow," Ariel said.

"I'll bet you're going to be happy to talk to Philly again." Roman knew he would be.

"Meow."

16

As Andre half dragged me down a slippery stone floor to the smugglers' cave, I began to feel as if none of what was happening was real. I had to be caught up in some kind of nightmare. Even under other circumstances, I doubt I would have enjoyed my little tour of a dank secret passage in an ancient castle. However, I would have awarded it five stars as a Halloween haunted-house experience.

The lantern Andre Magellan carried allowed us to see about three feet ahead—far enough that I saw rats scurry out of sight more than once. To add to the spooky atmosphere, there were the occasional cobwebs I had to brush off my face. Once, I was sure that an upset spider skittered across my shoulder and down my arm. But when I let out a scream, Andre's grip on my arm tightened, reminding me that rats and spiders were the least of my worries. What was happening to me was very real. I was on my way to a cave with a madman, and chances were good that another madman awaited us there.

I had to wonder if Roman had heard me say our destination.

Even more worrisome was what was going to happen when we reached that destination—especially if Carlo *was* waiting for us as Andre was predicting.

I was beginning to think that the passage would never

end, when a slab of stone blocked our path. Andre pushed against a panel and it slowly slid open. He tightened his grip on my arm and pulled me into the cave. The air was cold and damp, and I felt a sense of disorientation. The circle of light thrown by the lantern Andre was carrying offered little help. I had no idea where we were in the cave. Which way was the rope ladder Kit had used? Which way was the sea?

"This way." Andre pulled me with him to the right. We hadn't gone more than a few yards before a large boulder again blocked our path. There seemed to be some light on the other side. Andre shoved me ahead of him, and when I stepped around the rock, there was Carlo Ferrante.

Ferrante had staged the scene perfectly. But then I suppose that was part of the game. Dressed all in black, he sat cross-legged on a large flat stone. There was a lantern on one side of him and a package on the other. Carlo had slit the top open and a diamond necklace that made the one I was wearing look as if it had been created for a Barbie doll was draped over the side. He also had a large, deadly-looking gun in one of his hands.

Andre tightened his grip on my arm and pulled me with him toward Ferrante.

"Surprise," Carlo murmured.

"Actually, it's not a surprise at all." Andre's voice was tight but cool. "Tell him, Princess."

I had to swallow once hard to get rid of the lump of fear in my throat. "He said you'd be waiting for us."

"But the princess here—" Carlo paused to gesture with the gun in my direction "—she was a surprise, wasn't she?"

"Yes," Andre said. "Very clever of you. And having her wear the diamonds was a nice touch."

"I've always been better with the details. Admit it."

"I've always preferred to look at the big picture."

"If you'd been looking at the big picture, you never would have caused Michelangelo's death."

Andre sighed. "You're always harping on about that stupid horse. I offered to buy you another."

The two of them might have been talking about the weather or the score of their latest tennis or golf game. In the meantime, I was letting myself be trapped by a feeling of unreality again. I couldn't let that happen. I had to come up with some kind of escape plan. If Carlo had come here to kill Andre, then he wouldn't leave a witness behind. He'd kill me, too.

And since Andre had anticipated that Carlo would be in the cave, he must have a plan also. Plus, he had a gun tucked in his pocket. *Think.*

I'm here.

I blinked. *Ariel?*

Over here.

After checking to make sure that Carlo and Andre were still involved in reminiscing about their one-upmanship, I shifted my gaze into the darkness beyond the lanterns' glow. She was about fifteen feet away partially concealed by the boulder Andre and I had just circled around.

She sent me an image of Roman and I saw the darker shadow behind her. My heart leaped and then sank. He was facing two crazy men with guns who would spot him the minute he stepped into the light cast by the lanterns. If he was going to rescue me, I was going to have to help him.

"Where did you find her?" Andre asked.

Carlo laughed then, and the sound was as cold as the air that surrounded us in the cave.

"It was fate, I'm sure. But you had a hand in it, Andre. You hurt her cousin's cat. Her boyfriend got in touch with me because she wanted to save the animal. I know that you must find that hard to believe since you have no love for God's furry creatures. But she's here because you beat a cat named Caliban with a gun and left him trapped in this very cave. So you've played a part in your own downfall and in my perfect revenge. You have to appreciate the irony of that."

It was Andre's turn to laugh. It was a tight sound laced with anger. "Perfect revenge? Hardly. Do you think you've won this round merely because you sent someone here who looks like Isabella?"

"As a matter of fact, I know that I've won this round."

"How?" Andre's voice was becoming agitated now in direct contrast to the cool amusement in Carlo's voice.

He dropped my arm so that he could pace back and forth. Keeping my eyes on both men, I began to quietly inch myself toward Roman and Ariel.

Andre ran his hands through his hair.

Carlo watched him, an amused, complacent expression on his face. I had the distinct impression that his goading of Andre until the man's temper surfaced was part of their regular routine.

"You only gained access to this cave because I allowed it," Andre said. "My men have orders to use deadly force if you try to leave with those jewels."

"But I don't intend to leave with them."

Andre paused in his pacing, but his attention was riveted on Carlo. I risked taking a big step toward the back of the cave.

"What do you mean?" Andre asked.

Carlo gestured with his gun again. "Ask her."

I froze as both men turned toward me.

"She's working with the local police and Interpol to find evidence of your little fencing operation. I assume she's wearing a wire and the local police are already closing in. So you see, Andre, you're going to go to jail, and I am going to walk away with my recovered jewels."

"Bitch!" Andre drew his gun and aimed it at me.

Everything happened at once. Roman and Ariel raced into the light and Andre shifted his aim to Roman. The shot rang out just as Roman took me down in a hard tackle and Ariel leaped at Andre Magellan. Even though my ears were ringing from the shot, I heard Andre scream.

"Are you all right?" Roman asked. "Did he hit you?"

"I think I'm fine."

Roman scrambled to his feet. Andre Magellan was lying on his back, his hands over his face. Ariel stood next to him, licking her paws.

He hurt Caliban.

Roman dragged Andre to his feet and said solicitously, "Let me look at what she did to you."

When Andre dropped his hands, Roman punched him right in the face.

"Bravo. Well done."

Carlo had lain down his gun to applaud Roman. Roman whirled, dragged Carlo off the boulder and punched him in the face, too.

I was still staring, speechless, when Kit stepped into the glow of the lanterns with two uniformed policemen. "Damn! Looks like I missed all the fun."

DAWN WAS BREAKING when Inspector Ionescu joined our celebration on the terrace of the Villa Prospero. Demetria had shoved three tables together and we'd gathered around as a family. Ariel had a seat of honor at the head of the table flanked by Miranda and Alexi.

We greeted the inspector with the good news that Caliban was going to be all right. He had a simple fracture of his right front leg. The vet was going to keep him under observation for a few days, but he expected Ariel's brother to make a full recovery.

Ionescu had released Alexi at midnight when he'd taken Andre Magellan into the station house in Myrtos to book him.

"I also have some good news," Ionescu said as Alexi rose and added a chair for him right beside Miranda's. The inspector's tie was loose, his shirtsleeves rolled up. It was the only time I'd ever seen him look rumpled. But that meant he fit right in with the rest of us. Even though Kit and Roman and I had showered and changed when we'd returned from the Castello, we were still looking pretty bedraggled. The only exception was Miranda, who was, as usual, neat as a pin. And she had her glow back now that her son was home.

Kit, ever the diplomat, had chosen a time shortly after her reunion with Alexi to end our little masquerade and set Miranda straight about his and Roman's real identities. She'd surprised me by taking the news in stride, hugging both men and me. But perhaps Kit's presence had lifted the pressure on her to stand in for my family. I just felt relieved that one more lie was over.

I'd decided at some point during those frightening seconds in the cave when I'd seen the barrel of Andre's gun shift from me to Roman that I wanted to end *all* the lies.

Demetria poured the inspector a glass of wine, and I passed the plate of sandwiches.

"Do you have enough evidence to send Andre Magellan to jail?" I asked.

Ionescu spared me a small smile. "Thanks to you and your brother's state-of-the-art equipment—" he nodded toward Kit "—even the army of attorneys Magellan's parents will hire won't be able to keep him out of prison.

I'm not sure that we can pin Delos's murder on him. But I'm satisfied that he was behind it and that he tried to frame Alexi to keep him away from the caves."

Ionescu paused to sip his wine and then continued. "I'm hoping that when he faces the reality of prison, he'll give up the master thief he's been working with. Interpol wants to talk to him about that. But I advised that they wait until he's spent a few nights in one of my cells."

"It won't be the kind of five-star accommodations he's used to," Alexi said. "I can attest to that."

"You had five-star food, thanks to your mother," Ionescu pointed out.

"What bothers me," Roman said, "is that Carlo Ferrante is going to go free. It seems to me that he belongs behind bars, too."

This time Ionescu's smile wasn't small at all. "He may very well end up in jail for murder."

We all turned to stare at him.

"Who did he kill?" I asked.

"According to Magellan, Carlo Ferrante killed Isabella Carlini."

"But the police ruled her death an accident," Kit pointed out. "I had a contact in Scotland Yard check it out."

Ionescu sipped his wine. "It seems that bragging rights was a part of their game."

"That's exactly what they were doing in the cave before all hell broke loose," I said.

"After Isabella's fatal car crash, Carlo visited Andre's room to give him a blow-by-blow account of what he'd done. In addition to breaking the girl's heart and tampering with her brakes, he bragged to Andre that he'd slipped an overdose of a sleeping medication into her wine. Everything burned in the crash, but he'd hoped the police would find the bottle in her purse and rule it a suicide to torture Magellan even more. That confession will justify a charge of murder."

"But it will be just Andre's word against Carlo's," Kit said.

Ionescu shook his head. "It would have been except that Andre taped Carlo's confession."

Roman frowned. "Why didn't he turn it over to the police at the time?"

"Because of the game. He held it back so that he could use it at a time like this to prove that he was the superior game player."

"That's sick," Alexi commented.

Bad man.

"Ariel says that Carlo was a bad man, too," I said.

"Hear, hear." Roman raised his glass. "To Ariel who has saved Philly's and my life twice now."

We all toasted Ariel.

Ionescu rose. "I have to get back to the station."

"I'll walk you out," Miranda said.

Kit rose, too. "Alexi, can I bunk in with you?"

"Absolutely." The young man's face lit up. "I'll show you the way."

The moment they exited the terrace, I turned to Roman. "I know you have to be exhausted…"

"And you're not?"

"I need to talk to you. But not here." If I was going to do this, I had to do it right.

"Would you walk with me on the beach?"

The climb down to the beach seemed to take forever, giving Roman time to try to figure out what Philly wanted to say to him. But they'd nearly reached their destination, and he still wasn't sure.

He was a successful businessman. He knew how to read people. There was an energy and determination in her stride that told him she'd come to a decision. And he knew her well enough now to be fairly certain it had to do with the deal they'd made. Now that Kit was here, and he'd already relayed information about their adventure to the rest of their family back in San Francisco, Philly would want to clarify and settle things between them.

They were both on the same page there. He wanted to settle things also. He just hoped that they wanted to settle them the same way.

When they reached the promontory that separated them from the sandy white beach, Roman took her hand and they climbed over the wet rocks together. The sun hadn't risen far enough in the sky to dry them.

"I'm sorry for dragging you down here," she said. "This has to be the third time I've done it—first to show you Delos, then to try to find Ariel. It's just important that I tell you what I'm going to tell you here on the beach."

"No problem." But something in the seriousness of her tone had the nerves in Roman's stomach tightening. He made it a point to know his opponents in business. He could usually predict their reactions. Often he would even be able to foretell what their next move would be or what they would counteroffer. But Philly had been surprising him from the get-go.

First, she'd marched into his hospital room and proposed that they act on the attraction they felt for each other and have sex. Then she'd hightailed it off to Greece to find a lover. And she'd followed that by making him that other proposition on the terrace—the no-strings fling that would end once they returned to San Francisco.

So far he'd had a little trouble keeping up with her. But

that was going to stop. If she'd dragged him down here to throw him another curveball, he was going to catch it and throw it right back.

There had to be a way to figure out what was going on in her mind right now. Logically, they had two choices. One was to honor the deal they'd made, end their temporary sexual fling and try to go back to their old relationship.

Fat chance of that. Neither of them was going to forget what they'd shared together on Corfu. There was a magic here and it had ensnared both of them.

He knew what he wanted. The feelings that had been growing in him from the moment he'd run into her on that path and kissed her for the first time had come to full bloom. At some point he'd fallen in love with Philly Angelis. He just wasn't sure when.

Memories poured into his mind. Had it been when she'd shoved him on his ass? Or had it been on Stassis's jet when she'd turned into an imp and stripped for him? Another possibility was the time they'd escaped from that cave and she'd told him how terrible he'd looked and they'd lain there on the ground laughing like a couple of fools.

Or perhaps he'd been a goner ever since she'd walked into that hospital room and proposed they make love.

One thing he was clear about. He didn't want what they'd begun here in Greece to end. And Roman hoped she didn't want that, either. As she stopped and turned to face him, he thought he knew what she was going to say. She had that same look in her eyes that she'd had on the terrace two nights ago. She was going to tell him that she wanted to continue their sexual relationship.

"I don't want to lie anymore. And I think I've been lying to you from the beginning." She drew in a deep breath and let it out. "I don't want to have an affair with you."

If she'd intentionally meant to sucker punch him, she couldn't have been more successful. But this time Roman found his voice. "The hell you don't. Do you want me to prove you a liar?"

When he took two steps toward her, she backed away and held up her hands. "Wait. Let me finish. I figured it out while we were on Gianni's yacht. I *never* wanted to just have sex with you. It was all a lie—even when I said it in your hospital room. My mother and my aunt Cass met their true loves—the men they were meant to be with—on a beach in Greece. That's why I asked you to come here with me this morning. Even though we met before we came here, it's here in Greece that I figured out you're the one meant for me. I knew it the first night you made love to me. I love you, Roman, and I want much more than sex—even though it's been fabulous. I want to share a life with you. I want you to marry me."

This time the curveball hit him square in the chest, causing his heart to go into a free fall. His Philly was standing on a beach in Greece calmly proposing marriage to him. If he hadn't already fallen in love with her, he would now.

"I know marriage and commitment aren't what you want. You were clear on that. But I just don't want to lie to you anymore. I want you to know where I'm coming from."

"Philly…"

She held up her hand again. "You don't have to say anything. I just want there to be truth between us."

"Yes."

Now it was her turn to stare. He felt some satisfaction about that.

"Yes?"

Roman moved to her then, lifting her into his arms and swinging her around. "Yes, I'll marry you. Where's my ring?"

"Your ring?"

"I've never been proposed to before, but I've heard there's usually a ring involved."

She threw her arms around him and they were both still laughing when they spotted a large white bird soaring into the sky.

"Look!" She pointed at it. "I saw that bird the day I arrived and I knew it signaled the beginning of an adventure."

Roman set her down and framed her face in his hands. "We're about to begin another one, Philly. I love you, and I know that you're the one for me, too."

He kissed her as the white bird spiraled upward in the clear morning air.

Epilogue

"Two BEERS," Roman said to Spiro Angelis as he and Kit joined Nik and Theo at the bar of the Poseidon restaurant.

"Ah, Roman!" Spiro reached over the bar and thumped him on his shoulder. "Welcome back. We've missed you."

It felt good to be back, Roman thought. And coming to the Poseidon always felt like coming home. But it would feel better the next time he came—when he wouldn't have nerves knotted so tightly in his stomach. And a small box burning a hole in his pocket.

He shifted his gaze to the lobby of the restaurant, which was on the upper level overlooking the main seating area, but there was no sign of Philly.

When Spiro pushed a bottle of beer toward him, Roman took a long drink, then glanced around the large dining room. The women, including his two sisters, Sadie and Juliana, Nik's and Kit's fiancées, J.C. and Drew, as well as Cass and Helena Angelis, were already seated at one end of a long table, studying lists and what looked to be sketches.

"Wedding business," Kit explained. "Now that they've pretty well organized Nik and J.C.'s Thanksgiving extravaganza, I think Drew is sketching designs for Sadie. Theirs will have a Christmas theme."

"What about a dress for herself?" Theo asked.

Kit grinned. "All taken care of. It was her first design. She fell in love with it, and now that she's fallen for me, too, she gets to wear it on Valentine's Day."

All the talk of weddings was just making Roman more nervous. At the other end of the table, about as far from the women as they could get, sat Roman's father, Mario, Juliana's fiancé, Paulo Carlucci, and Mason Leone. Roman had invited them all. And in spite of the fact that everyone seemed occupied, they knew something was up. He and Philly had only been back from Greece for a day, but he'd felt an urgent need to take care of this.

Everyone was here except for Philly. She'd left a message on his cell that she'd be a little late. Roman took another swig of his beer, then he turned to face Philly's father.

"I have something to say."

Spiro grinned at him. "So, say it."

Dammit. It shouldn't be so hard to get the words out. He'd had less trouble when he and his father had negotiated a very tricky land deal with the Carluccis, who had been the Capulets to their Montagues since both families had come over from the old country. But then he'd never envisioned himself in this situation. This wasn't supposed to have been in the cards for him.

Roman cleared his throat. "I want permission to ask your daughter to marry me."

There was a beat of silence before Spiro circled out from behind the bar and enveloped him in a huge hug. "It's about time. She's been waiting for you for a long while, I think." He turned and waved the rest of the family over. "We're going to have another wedding."

Roman glanced at Kit and his brothers. They, too, were grinning from ear to ear.

Kit raised his glass. "To more weddings."

"It was the trip to Greece, wasn't it?" Spiro asked. "We Angelises have a weakness for falling in love in Greece. It's the equivalent of Cupid's arrow." Spiro thumped his chest with his fist.

There was a sudden commotion at the head of the stairs and Philly barreled down them. When she reached Roman at the bar, she was out of breath. But she threw her arms around him and hugged him hard.

"I've got something for you. That's why I was late."

"Philly, I—"

"No." She raised a hand to cut him off. "Let me finish first." Then she pulled a small box out of her pocket and opened it. "Here's the ring. Now we can make it official. Will you marry me, Roman?"

He should have known she'd do this. Maybe when they were married thirty or forty years, he'd be able to predict her.

"That's my girl," Spiro said proudly.

Roman took the small box out of his pocket and opened it. "I'll marry you if you'll marry me."

She kissed him then, and around them the entire family broke into applause.

CASS STOOD on the fringe of her family and for once saw only the present—all four of her sister Penelope's children had found their true loves. Tears pricked at the back of her eyes. Perhaps her son Dino would be next. In his last letter he'd said that he might make it home for the holidays and Theo's wedding. Lord, how she missed him.

Mason slipped his hand into hers. "Do you want me to take you to Greece, Cassandra?"

She turned to him then. "No. I don't have to go to Greece. I've made my decision, Mason. Or you've helped me make it."

"Good." He brushed his mouth briefly over hers, before they turned to watch Roman and Philly exchange rings.

* * * * *

Don't miss Dino Angelis's story,
coming in December!

The Colton family is back!
Enjoy a sneak preview of
COLTON'S SECRET SERVICE by Marie Ferrarella,
part of THE COLTONS: FAMILY FIRST *miniseries.*

Available from Silhouette Romantic Suspense
in September 2008.

He cautioned himself to be leery. He was human and he'd been conned before. But never by anyone nearly so attractive. Never by anyone he'd felt so attracted to.

In her defense, Nick supposed that Georgie could actually be telling him the truth. That she was a victim in all this. He had his people back in California checking her out, to make sure she was who she said she was and had, as she claimed, not even been near a computer but on the road these last few months that the threats had been made.

In the meantime, he was doing his own checking out. Up close and exceedingly personal. So personal he could feel his blood stirring.

It had been a long time since he'd thought of himself as anything other than a law enforcement agent of one type or other. But Georgeann Grady made him remember that beneath the oaths he had taken and his devotion to duty, there beat the heart of a man.

A man who'd been far too long without the touch of a woman.

He watched as the light from the fireplace caressed the outline of Georgie's small, trim, jean-clad body as she moved about the rustic living room that could have easily come off the set of a Hollywood Western. Except that it was genuine.

As genuine as she claimed to be?

Something inside of him hoped so.

He wasn't supposed to be taking sides. His only interest in being here was to guarantee Senator Joe Colton's safety as the latter continued to make his bid for the presidency. Everything else was supposed to be secondary, but, Nick had to silently admit, that was just a wee bit hard to remember right now.

Earlier, before she'd put her precocious handful of a daughter to bed, Georgie had fed his appetite by whipping up some kind of a delicious concoction out of the vegetables she'd pulled from her garden. Vegetables that, by all rights, should have been withered and dried. She'd mentioned that a friend came by on occasion to weed and tend it. Still, it surprised him that somehow she'd managed to make something mouthwatering out of it.

Almost as mouthwatering as she looked to him right at this moment.

Again, he was reminded of the appetite that hadn't been fed, hadn't been satisfied.

And wasn't going to be, Nick sternly told himself. At least not now. Maybe later, when things took on a more definite shape and all the questions in his head were answered to his satisfaction, there would be time to explore this feeling. This woman. But not now.

Damn it.

"Sorry about the lack of light," Georgie said, breaking into his train of thought as she turned around to face him. If she noticed the way he was looking at her, she gave no indication. "But I don't see a point in paying for electricity if I'm not going to be here. Besides, Emmie really enjoys camping out. She likes roughing it."

"And you?" Nick asked, moving closer to her, so close that a whisper would have trouble fitting in. "What do you like?"

The very breath stopped in Georgie's throat as she looked up at him.

"I think you've got a fair shot of guessing that one," she told him softly.

* * * * *

Be sure to look for
COLTON'S SECRET SERVICE
and the other following titles from
THE COLTONS: FAMILY FIRST *miniseries:*

RANCHER'S REDEMPTION
by Beth Cornelison
THE SHERIFF'S AMNESIAC BRIDE
by Linda Conrad
SOLDIER'S SECRET CHILD
by Caridad Piñeiro
BABY'S WATCH
by Justine Davis
A HERO OF HER OWN
by Carla Cassidy

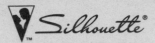

Romantic
SUSPENSE

Sparked *by Danger*, *Fueled by Passion.*

The Coltons Are Back!

Marie Ferrarella
Colton's Secret Service

The Coltons: Family First

On a mission to protect a senator, Secret Service agent
Nick Sheffield tracks down a threatening message only
to discover Georgie Gradie Colton, a rodeo-riding single
mom, who insists on her innocence. Nick is instantly
taken with the feisty redhead, but vows not to let his
feelings interfere with his mission. Now he must figure
out if this woman is conning him or if he can trust her
and the passion they share....

Available September wherever books are sold.

Look for upcoming Colton titles
from Silhouette Romantic Suspense:

RANCHER'S REDEMPTION by Beth Cornelison, Available October
THE SHERIFF'S AMNESIAC BRIDE by Linda Conrad, Available November
SOLDIER'S SECRET CHILD by Caridad Piñeiro, Available December
BABY'S WATCH by Justine Davis, Available January 2009
A HERO OF HER OWN by Carla Cassidy, Available February 2009

Visit Silhouette Books at www.eHarlequin.com   SRS27598

HARLEQUIN
More Than Words

"The transformation is the Cinderella story over and over again."

—**Ruth Renwick,** real-life heroine

*Ruth Renwick is a Harlequin More Than Words
award winner and the founder of **Inside The Dream.***

Discover your inner heroine!

SUPPORTING CAUSES OF CONCERN TO WOMEN **HARLEQUIN**
WWW.HARLEQUINMORETHANWORDS.COM

MTW07RRI

REQUEST YOUR FREE BOOKS!

2 FREE NOVELS
PLUS 2
FREE GIFTS!

HARLEQUIN®

Blaze™

Red-hot reads!

YES! Please send me 2 FREE Harlequin® Blaze™ novels and my 2 FREE gifts (gifts are worth about $10). After receiving them, if I don't wish to receive any more books, I can return the shipping statement marked "cancel". If I don't cancel, I will receive 6 brand-new novels every month and be billed just $4.24 per book in the U.S. or $4.71 per book in Canada, plus 25¢ shipping and handling per book and applicable taxes, if any*. That's a savings of 15% or more off the cover price! I understand that accepting the 2 free books and gifts places me under no obligation to buy anything. I can always return a shipment and cancel at any time. Even if I never buy another book, the two free books and gifts are mine to keep forever.

151 HDN ERVA   351 HDN ERUX

Name _____ (PLEASE PRINT) _____

Address _____ Apt. # _____

City _____ State/Prov. _____ Zip/Postal Code _____

Signature (if under 18, a parent or guardian must sign)

Mail to the Harlequin Reader Service:
IN U.S.A.: P.O. Box 1867, Buffalo, NY 14240-1867
IN CANADA: P.O. Box 609, Fort Erie, Ontario L2A 5X3

Not valid to current subscribers of Harlequin Blaze books.

Want to try two free books from another line?
Call 1-800-873-8635 or visit www.morefreebooks.com.

* Terms and prices subject to change without notice. N.Y. residents add applicable sales tax. Canadian residents will be charged applicable provincial taxes and GST. Offer not valid in Quebec. This offer is limited to one order per household. All orders subject to approval. Credit or debit balances in a customer's account(s) may be offset by any other outstanding balance owed by or to the customer. Please allow 4 to 6 weeks for delivery. Offer available while quantities last.

Your Privacy: Harlequin Books is committed to protecting your privacy. Our Privacy Policy is available online at www.eHarlequin.com or upon request from the Reader Service. From time to time we make our lists of customers available to reputable third parties who may have a product or service of interest to you. If you would prefer we not share your name and address, please check here. ☐

HB08R

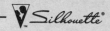

SPECIAL EDITION™

NEW YORK TIMES
BESTSELLING AUTHOR

DIANA PALMER

A brand-new Long, Tall Texans novel

HEART OF STONE

Feeling unwanted and unloved, Keely returns
to Jacobsville and to Boone Sinclair, a rancher
troubled by his own past. Boone has always
seemed reserved, but now Keely discovers a
sensuality with him that quickly turns to love. Can
they each see past their own scars to let love in?

Available September 2008
wherever you buy books.

HARLEQUIN®

Blaze™

COMING NEXT MONTH

#417 ALL OR NOTHING Debbi Rawlins
Posing undercover as a Hollywood producer to investigate thefts at the
St. Martine hotel has good ol' Texas cowboy Chase Culver sweatin' under
his Stetson. All the up-close contact with the hotel's gorgeous personal trainer
Dana McGuire isn't helping either, and she's his prime suspect!

#418 RISQUÉ BUSINESS Tawny Weber
Blush
Delaney Connor can't believe the way her life has changed! The former mousy
college professor is now a TV celebrity, thanks to a makeover and a talent for
reviewing pop fiction. She's at the top of her game—until bad boy author
Nick Angel tests her skills both as a reviewer…and as a woman.

#419 AT HER PLEASURE Cindi Myers
Who knew science could be so…sensual? For researcher Ian Marshall his
summer of solitude on an uninhabited desert island becomes much more
interesting with the arrival of Nicole Howard. And when she offers a no-
strings-attached affair, how can he resist?

#420 SEX & THE SINGLE SEAL Jamie Sobrato
Forbidden Fantasies
When something feels this taboo, it has to be right. That's how Lieutenant
Commander Kyle Thomas explains her against-the-rules lust for her
subordinate Drew MacLeod. So when she finally gets the chance to seduce
him, nothing will stand in her way.

#421 LIVE AND YEARN Kelley St. John
The Sexth Sense, Bk. 6
When Charles Roussel runs into former flame Nanette Vicknair, he knows
she's still mad at his betrayal years ago. But before he can explain, he's cast
adrift in a nether world, neither alive nor dead. Except, that is, in her bed every
night. There he proves to her that he's truly the man of her dreams!

#422 OVERNIGHT SENSATION Karen Foley
Actress Ivy James has just hit the big time. She's earned the lead role in a
blockbuster movie based on the true-to-life sexual experiences of war hero
Garrett Stokes, and her costar is one of Hollywood's biggest and brightest
actors. The problem? The only one she wants to share a bed with—on-screen
and off—is Garrett himself!

HBCNM0808

www.eHarlequin.com